CALABASH
PARKWAY

A Novel by Brenda Chester DoHarris,

Author of

The Coloured Girl in the Ring

Tantaria Press,
Bowie, Maryland
www.TantariaPress.com

All incidents related herein are entirely fictitious. Any resemblance of this novel's characters to persons living or dead is purely coincidental.

ISBN No. 0-9770728-0-0
Library of Congress Copyright   2005

For Rebecca, my mother
—my first love—
and for my "undocumented" sisters and brothers
who languish in limbo

Dedicated to the memory of my father, Clement Vincent "C.V." Chester, whose hands, in Guyana's hinterland, saved lives and eased new life into the world; who fought bravely against his own 'dying of the light'; but who now joyfully sings and dances with the ancestors

THE NEW COLOSSUS

Not like the brazen giant of Greek fame,
With conquering limbs astride from land to land;
Here at our sea-washed, sunset gates shall stand
A mighty woman with a torch, whose flame
Is the imprisoned lightning, and her name,
Mother of Exiles. From her beacon-hand
Glows world-wide welcome; her mild eyes command
The air-bridged harbor that twin cities frame.
"Keep, ancient lands, your storied pomp!" cries she
With silent lips. "Give me your tired, your poor,
Your huddled masses yearning to breathe free,
The wretched refuse of your teeming shore.
Send these, the homeless, tempest-tost to me,
I lift my lamp beside the golden door!"

**Emma Lazarus' Sonnet to the Statue of Liberty
New York City, 1883**

AFTER ONE YEAR

After today, how shall I speak with you?
Those miseries I know you cultivate
Are mine as well as yours, or do you think
The impartial bullock cares whose land is ploughed?

I know this city much as well as you do,
the ways leading to brothels and those dooms
dwelling in them, as in our lives they dwell.
So jail me quickly, clang the illiterate door
If freedom writes no happier alphabet.

Old hanging ground is still green playing field
Smooth cemetery proud garden of tall flowers.
But in your secret gables real bats fly
Mocking great dreams that give the soul no peace,
And everywhere wrong deeds are being done.

Rude citizen! Think you I do not know
That love is stammered, hate is shouted out
In every human city in this world?
Men murder men, as men must murder men,
To build their shining governments of the damned.

**Martin Carter, Guyanese National Poet,
from *Jail Me Quickly*, 1964**

Acknowledgements

My deep appreciation goes to the following:

My editors, Sandra Seeraj and Shansa Barrow, who worked patiently and assiduously with the text;

Dawn Affiliated Services for the cover and book design;

Peggy David for helping me *wrastle wid de title*;

Rochika Chaudhry for generously sharing with me information on Hindu mythological lore;

Billy Braithwaite, Pansy Marshall Brown, Paul Chester, Jacqueline Cholmondeley, Neila Cholmondeley, Eusi Kwayana, Jacob Winston Wills and Maxford Wolfe, all of whose cultural memory remains unassailable and who always keep me mindful of things Guyanese;

and Bishops' High School of Guyana alumni for their constant, unwavering support.

Prologue

If in the relation of this tale, I do not tell you the whole truth, bear with me, for I would not have done so intentionally. You see, the stuff of this story is stitched with the threads of memory—mine and that of others—we who pass like ghosts through changing seasons on alien shores. If in my telling, you find that I have sometimes unraveled the hem of truth, consider that sometimes flawed fact may be no less engaging than faultless fiction.

It was Manhattan, December 1979. As the train approached Jay Street/Borough Hall station, she rose slowly from her seat, going with the clackety motion and walking down the passage between the seats like a sailor on a heaving deck. The flash of her face in my mind and the roar of the train jolted my memory. It was 'Gatha. I had last seen her fifteen years before in 1964, when I had left what was then British Guiana to study in Washington, D.C. In the Guyanese village of Kitty where we had grown up, she had worked as a seamstress, a young woman who had made my school uniforms in my elementary and high school years. Eustace, her lover and a village policeman, had jilted her in favor of another woman, Shirley. Left devastated and pregnant, it seemed that she would go mad. Barely eating or sleeping for months, she abandoned herself to despair and relinquished the care of her children to relatives. The child that she carried, a little girl, was stillborn. Then, in a shocking turn of events, Eustace killed his new lover, Shirley, whom he suspected of being unfaithful. The next day he committed suicide by hurling himself in the path of a train that was speeding down the East Coast to the capital, Georgetown. 'Gatha slowly pulled herself together, and by the time I left British Guiana, she had resumed her dressmaking business and started a relationship with a bus driver named Leon.

For me, in the ensuing years, Eustace's actions and their senselessness made the rumble-rattle of a train a poignant, roaring reminder of the frightening human potential for destructiveness. I marveled at 'Gatha's resiliency in being able to recover from her despair. At first, through postcards from Washington, D.C.—the Jefferson Memorial framed by cherry blossoms, the White House shrouded in snow, Lincoln sitting long-legged and seemingly benign—people and places that were so removed from her own experience in the hot, stifling village, I kept in touch with 'Gatha. She would write me in her slanting, slightly awkward hand, regaling me with village gossip—who died, who got married, who "t'row 'way baby," who had died. Eventually, the demands of student life and the rigors of adjusting to a new environment took priority over my interest in the affairs of a distant village that over time, had receded in my consciousness but never left it. The frequency of our contact dwindled into nothing, but I always remembered her courage because, apart from my mother, she was my first example of a woman's fierce determination to ride the waves of grief and not to be submerged by them.

PART ONE
"Hungry daag a nyam kyalabash."

Guyanese Creole Saying

CHAPTER ONE

The train ground to a halt, its brakes screaming shrilly like a dog in pain.

" 'Gatha?" I called-questioned above the grating noise of metal.

" 'Gatha?"

" 'Gatha!"

I rose and started moving to meet her.

She stopped in the train's doorway, her progress seemingly blocked by the sound of her name then glanced in my direction, recognition swiftly sweeping her face. In the seconds that the train's open door allowed her, she hovered in the crack of indecision. After all, she must have wanted to get home and out of the cold as quickly as she could. She seemed exhausted, wearing that look of faintly greasy fatigue that creeps over the faces of New York strap-hangers after the long, long hours. Every day Caribbean people identified each other in the grimy, clackety-clack underground across waves of swaying strangers in a subterranean, graffiti-smeared world where recollection sometimes came slowly, and reunions were all too brief or avoided entirely—"Isn't dat Beryl's son, Leroy, sittin' dung ovuh dare near dat Hasidic Jew? Leroy, de one who couldn' keep 'is hands to 'imself. Leroy who look like 'e was out to make a baby wid ev'ry village gyurl dat smile at 'im. A wonda if 'e jus' come. *A wonda wheh 'e workin'.* "

She hesitated at the door. She could step out onto the platform and be swallowed up in the cold wind of the Brooklyn night, lost to the friendship we once knew, or she could remain

1

and renew old acquaintance. It seemed that the decision had already been already made for her. The train door slammed shut, and we rushed to embrace each other as the train pulled out.

Since that night so many years ago, I have often wondered at the destiny that drew us together again. Had she simply waved in recognition, quickly stepped off onto the platform, and gone about her business, I would not now be telling you this story. How strange that I should run into her after so many years, a Kitty village face from Lamaha Street of many years past, ever so slightly out of place in the gritty, rumbling, metropolitan underbelly of New York. Over the years since we reconnected on that wintry night in 1979, we remained in close touch until years later when fate would again take a hand.

Before we met on the train, I realized that so much separated me from the village that I had left behind, the place that had formed me so many years before, so many miles away. I was then a graduate student at Columbia University, working towards a degree in an atmosphere that was intellectually stimulating but culturally distant from Kitty. I was studying on the upper West Side where many of my professors were famous in American life but where some in the academy had only a vague idea of Guyana's existence and many could have cared less. Sometimes I would leave the campus and walk the streets of the surrounding Spanish Harlem just to hear and feel the sounds and rhythms of Spanish ethnicity, to remind myself of a way of life that I had left behind and of a cultural identity that I was determined to hold on to.

"… No, not Ghana. Guyana… Yes, yes, Guyana. You see—Ghana is in Africa. We are in South America. Yes, yes. Guyana. No. Not Guinea. Guyana. Guyana with a 'y' not an 'i.' Yes, we used to be Guiana with an 'i,' but now we are Guyana with a 'y.' "

"South America? Are you sure? Are you *really* sure? Don't all those folks down there speak Spanish? Well... ? don't they?"

She called my name, and we were hugging, the years falling away and taking us back to the last time in late August 1964, when we had embraced like this at Atkinson Airport Then, with the country embroiled in race riots, we had vowed to keep in touch, each of us secretly knowing that time would wipe clean memory's slate of promises.

"What are you doing in New York? How long have you been here?" I asked, other questions crowding my mind before I had a chance to ask them.

"What about Leon?"

"How are the children?"

She started to answer, and we were off again to the next stop, almost falling against each other in the jolting motion.

"Leon and the kids are fine. We got married the year after you left. Let's get off at the next stop," she said. "I know a Caribbean place nare dare where we could talk."

She had not lost her Guyanese accent or her disposition to Creolese. When I first knew her in Guyana, she was a woman in her early twenties. At the time of this meeting, she must have been about thirty-seven, and in her eyes, I saw the maturity and knowing, the unwritten text of unfolding courage. Winter was slowly settling on New York. It hung like a cold, invisible shroud over Brooklyn's tawdry little Asian green groceries, Caribbean bakeries, travel agencies, hair dressing salons, card reading parlors, smoke shops and shipping businesses. It settled over fruit stands with their apples that never *smelled* sweet like those we were accustomed to in the warm Christmases of our "small days." It froze our hopes for change in the country we had left behind. The cold wind moved inside our collars, tickled our ears, flicked fragments of newspapers up and down the street where overflowing

3

garbage cans awaited the next day's noisy arrival of city trash-haulers. It seemed that the years had not intervened and we picked up right where we had left off in 1964, one of the bloodiest years in our country's history.

We had gotten off at the Nevins stop and walked to a nearby Caribbean café where we could duck indoors from the cold and talk. From the list of items displayed on a large board that mentioned bus-up-shut, ginger beer, butter flap, cook-up, we ordered *mauby*, the bitter Guyanese brew.

Once when visiting Guyana in the early seventies, I inquired about her, Leon and the children. Her little cottage in Kitty had been torn down. That place where village women met and gossiped, where she made brides' dresses, children's school uniforms (including mine), and sensible cotton frocks for the wives of expatriate diplomats, was now replaced by a mechanic's shop. There, amid a few battered, rusty hulks of cars, old tires and motor bikes, *limers* and some mechanics drank *Bank's*, smoked *Broadway* cigarettes, cursed, spat, *called off* passing women, talked about women, spat, *tackled* women, played noisy dominoes, and occasionally turned to the business of fixing cars. A young man with a matchstick dangling carelessly from between nicotine-stained lips told me that 'Gatha and her family had moved to another area of Kitty. A grease-stained mechanic lifted his head from under the hood of a car to say no, he was sure dat deh livin' wid her aunt in Kingston; Miss Ada and Miss Edna, two Black pudding women in Kitty whom I had known since childhood, said no, dat not true. Dat *certainly* not true. Deh livin' wid relatives in Beterverwagting. Before I could locate them, it was time for me to leave again.

After Eustace jilted 'Gatha, grief settled over her, dark-gray-dense as a Berbice storm cloud at twilight, only to descend later in a rain of self-neglect. She had lost them both—Eustace whom she still silently loved in spite of his desertion

4

and her baby girl. 'Gatha had first seen her right after the village midwife had eased her from the womb, the umbilical cord wrapped tightly around her neck, her tiny body covered in the vernix of birth. In the months following, 'Gatha would hear a baby's cry in the dark, and she would sit bolt upright in bed, listening, hungry for the infant, her empty arms outstretched. Stumbling in the gray gloom, she would strain to hear the sound again... in the empty silence thick with the nauseating smell of mosquito destroyer. In her dreams, she would see the infant, the umbilical cord circling her neck, her eyes frozen in a death stare. Then 'Gatha would feel herself choking and wake sweating, gasping for air, her fingers prying at her own throat.

Even as she began to heal, to feel the pangs of desire creeping up the insides of her legs and into her belly again, to sense her breasts' stirring for a man's touch, she knew that life would never be the same, that the scars would always be there, hard over the hurt. She resumed life, sewing for the city's Canadian diplomatic wives and others. Then she met Leon.

He lacked Eustace's toughness and treated her with a gentleness and generosity that yet spoke of strength that was rarely seen in the other men she knew in the village. During the 1962 riots, he left the Transport and Harbours Department where he had worked as a bus driver and began driving an old, battered third-hand Morris Minor taxi. She had known him while he drove the bus, and after Eustace's death, their friendship developed from their frequent meetings when she was a passenger. He shared what little he had with her and her two small boys, Eustace's sons. Gradually she found herself being drawn to this large, clumsy, but gentle man whose heart was big enough to accommodate her and her children. He gave up the small room he was renting in Pike Street and moved into her cottage. Sometimes he would take them all in the taxi to the Brown Betty snack bar and buy them ice cream and giant-sized twenty-five cent hamburgers. Within a year, he proposed over a chicken-in-the-rough and cream soda dinner at the Rendezvous Restaurant on Robb Street in the city's warm heart.

"Ah really love yuh, gyurl," he said in a voice made hoarse by emotion. "Ah t'ink we kyan mek it. Gi'e me a chance. Ah love you an' de chirren an' Ah believe you love me too. Leh me *write home* to Miss Evangeline fuh you." Miss Evangeline, 'Gatha's great-aunt, had raised her from the age of six when 'Gatha's mother had died of malaria.

While 'Gatha liked him immensely, she did not love Leon, certainly not as she thought she had Eustace. But who knew what love was? Look at the grief that 'love' had led her to with *him*. She thought that time would take care of her feelings and that she could grow to care deeply for Leon. He did not stir her passion as Eustace once had, but she had to be practical. There was more to life than having one's heart beat fast for a man. Right then, her boys were most important. She recognized that they needed a male figure in their lives, one who was so strong in his skin and spirit that he was not afraid to be gentle. Here was such a man willing to give what she had yearned for from Eustace, yet she was foolishly allowing herself to have qualms. She slowly reached across the table, placing her small rough hand inside his large palm.

"I love you too, darlin'," she lied with as much conviction as she could muster. "I *will* marry you, an' yuh doan need to write Aunt Evangeline. *I'se me own big woman.*"

However, despite 'Gatha's protestation of maturity and independence, Leon insisted that he write Miss Evangeline to signal his intention of marrying her niece. In 1965, he and 'Gatha were married at the Anglican church of St. James-the-Less in Kitty. The village gossips hung around the church door and whispered about 'Gatha's good fortune after all her grief.

"Eh, eh, chile. Eh, eh," said Miss Joycie to Mama Rose, the obeah woman. "It look like God finally smile on dis pore gyurl."

"It seem like she din need yuh help dis time." Miss Joycie added this last bit a little derisively because the village *spit press* knew that 'Gatha had once unsuccessfully resorted to Mama Rose's 'supernatural powers' in the hope of inducing Eustace to marry her.

"Maybe not," Mama Rose flung back calmly and ominously at Miss Joycie. "Maybe not. But remember, *yuh nuh dead yet, cuckabeh nah pass you...* "

Seven years after their marriage, after the face of the dead baby girl had begun to fade from her memory, after she lost hope that she would conceive any children by Leon, they had identical twin girls, Precious and Princess. The girls came just when 'Gatha felt sure that she would never feel the thrill of pure love for him which she had initially thought that the passage of time would provide her. They came screaming into the world just when she was certain that she would have to settle for simply liking and admiring him. In the euphoria immediately following the girls' birth, she thought that he might yet fill the nagging emptiness in her, rouse the sleeping passion in her belly. For his part, he was smitten with what he called "*all my gyurls.*" He boasted to his friends at the lodge hall on Durban Street, those who had *tantalized* him in earlier years about his 'firing blanks,' that the appearance of twins, even though they were girls, was a sure indication of his virility.

By early 1979, the bright promises of political independence had lost their luster. The shadow of political tyranny and economic malaise loomed over the country. In fear of reprisal, people were careful of their utterances—what they said and to whom— as dissent was equated with disloyalty. Shortages of essential items made daily life difficult. Soon it became impossible for Leon to find spare parts and tires so necessary for him to earn a living driving the taxi. As life got harder for working class Guyanese in general, some of 'Gatha's clients drifted away. Her expatriate patrons now bought their clothes overseas. Emigration stole others away. Were it not for Eunice Griffith and other local long-time faithfuls, 'Gatha's sewing business would have disappeared.

Eunice Griffith was seventyish, single, childless—a woman of some means. In the early nineteen-thirties, she had been a young country midwife in the village of Fellowship on the West Coast of the Demerara. Through prudent management of her small income (and between infant deliveries), she started rearing chickens and soon developed a tiny poultry farm, which later evolved into a larger, successful enterprise that she called Payne's Poultry. At first, this name caused the Fellowship women to snigger because they felt she was *playin' great, smellin' sheself,* displaying unseemly arrogance for a woman. Yet it was to her coops that they went when they needed to buy chickens for their Christmas and Easter tables and for other occasions. No one ever referred to her *full mout'* as "Eunice." Her very demeanor discouraged familiarity. She was either "Miss Eunice" or "Miss Payne," thank you very much.

Living alone in a cottage she inherited from her parents who had died just before she was twenty, Eunice had had several admirers at social events like the *dajuneers* she attended at places like Den Amstel and Parika on the West Coast. Yet she was never interested in marriage, being single-mindedly (and unusually, for her time) driven by a desire for independence and financial security in her own right. The village men bored her. It was not that she suspected that they were not her intellectual equals. She was convinced of it.

At about forty, she moved to a spacious expensively redecorated house in Kingston, a suburb of Georgetown. Over the years she spent there, she increased her wealth by buying properties in Georgetown, many of which she either rented or profitably resold. In her business transactions, she had become known for a cool shrewdness that gained her respect among the city's business people, most of whom were men.

Among her servants and poor tenants in the "Warlock," Federation Yard and Tiger Bay areas of the city, she was feared and detested. So Eunice became independent at a time when the masses of women in Georgetown evaded penury by attaching themselves to men, either by marriage or common law arrangements. Many others struggled as poorly paid nurses, teachers, civil servants, or service workers.

Eunice was a tall, thin, erect woman, strict with her servants and tradespeople she employed. She seldom smiled and over the years, her facial features settled into a stiff resignation. She always told people who asked about her success (and tenants who attempted to play fast and loose with her rent) that in her climb, it was always *she one and God.* *"Me one and God,"* she would emphasize. "Not a mother, not a father, not a fren'."

In her own gruff way, she was kind to 'Gatha and her children, sometimes paying her generously in excess for the dresses 'Gatha made her. On occasion, during the August holidays, she had hired 'Gatha's two older sons as yard boys and general helpers and taken a keen personal interest in their education. Soon, 'Gatha became not only Eunice's seamstress but her confidante. Over the years that 'Gatha sewed her dresses, Eunice made her privy to information related to her business affairs. Sometimes 'Gatha accompanied her to court when she sued tenants who were in arrears.

She would advise 'Gatha, "Take care of yuhself, gyurl. Tek care of yuhself! Tek yuhself seriously. Doan trus' no man to tek care of you. Look to yuhself an' yuh chirren."

But 'Gatha would not allow herself to be drawn under Eunice's hard shell, harder, thicker than that of an Essequibo River turtle at low tide on a moonlit night. Even though 'Gatha sometimes felt that something was missing in her relationship with Leon, she would listen to Miss Eunice, but she *would n' pick 'er teet'.* She would make noises of agreement but she *would n' pick 'er teet'.* Even with 'Gatha, Eunice's mild amiability could change suddenly if a dress did not fit just right, if this flare skirt drooped, if that seam was not straight.

A diagnosis of uterine cancer early in 1979 would leave Eunice devastated. For once, the confidence on which she had founded her drive for personal independence was rocked. She decided that she would go to her god-daughter, Celeste, in New York and see a physician there for a second opinion. However, she needed someone to accompany her, someone whom she could think of as a friend but who would also be hired help in the day to day exertions which she was beginning to find difficult. It did not take her long to decide that 'Gatha was the ideal companion for this mission.

CHAPTER TWO

For 'Gatha and Leon in 1979, life grew more difficult. Apart from shortages of essential items such as flour, gasoline, cooking oil, milk, soap and even toilet paper, health and other necessary services were deteriorating rapidly. Now routine, failures of the electricity supply made ongoing food and other refrigeration impossible. The city morticians had trouble preserving the dead. Garbage services in the city were erratic and sometimes non-existent. Daily breakdowns in the water supply affected the quality and availability of water for consumption and washing. When the rains came, flooding sometimes threatened life.

Intensifying the situation, the government stifled dissent, denying newsprint to opposition newspapers; removing opposition broadcasters from the two government-owned and controlled radio stations; resorting to organized thugs who physically attacked anti-government speakers at political meetings on Bourda Green or elsewhere in the city; and firing or denying employment to opponents of the regime. Trade unionists who tried to instigate strikes were themselves threatened or attacked. The rule of law took a back seat as political opponents were snatched off the streets, tortured and held for days without being charged. The names Ayangana and Eve Leary assumed ominous connotations. One grew cautious about what one said and to whom one said it. Afta rall, *every skin teet' na laugh.* Now frightened, despairing, and vulnerable, some people started hoping for relief from the outside, "from up north," as the *limers* called the powerful shadow that they saw in America.

"Oh," they said, with false certainty. "Eventually de Americans will step in. Deh will *have* to. If dey don't, den Englan' will have to."

No one told them that America was preoccupied with other more important dictatorships, some of its own creation, regimes which affected America's "national interest" far more seriously than Guyana's did.

As the country lurched on politically and economically, the personal hardships on families increased. Repeatedly in 1979, one heard that it was the International Year of the Child, but it was also one of economic austerity that most adversely affected children. Precious and Princess, Leon's and 'Gatha's seven-year old twins, were asthmatic and their parents could ill afford medicine and professional care. Tires and spare parts for the taxi were in short supply, and because Leon also used the Morris Minor to transport the family around Kitty and Georgetown, the wear and tear on the old car was greater than would ordinarily have been the case. More people were buying ready-made imported dresses and other clothing that the growing bands of traders were bringing into the country. Therefore, 'Gatha's dressmaking business was badly affected. While the two older boys scrambled to get work in their spare time, the money was still not enough for the family's rising expenses. Delivered by the 'small boy' who stood insolently picking his teeth outside her door, Eunice's summons could not have come at a more opportune time.

Eunice had hoped that her money would insure her against the cervical cancer that gnawed at her hope as it did her womb. Speaking euphemistically, the doctors told her to expect "some discomfort." But everyone with a grain of sense knew that in medical lingo "some discomfort" could mean serious pain. By 1979, the movement of disenchanted professional people out of the country had begun, and in spite of her willingness and ability to pay, Eunice's doctor was hard pressed and could not give her the extra attention she desperately needed. With the shortage of drugs and medical equipment, doctors were turning the spotlight of their concern on the treatable. Medical waiting rooms were crammed with the sick, some sitting so long that they fell asleep with their mouths wide open as the flies buzzed around them in the heat.

True enough, Eunice's god-daughter in Brooklyn would send her the occasional barrel—mostly some delicacies and clothing. But there were other necessities like good personal and public health that eluded the "barrel" culture, that could not be shipped in to the country. As a younger, healthier woman, she had looked pityingly—and a little smugly—at the sickly poor, feeling confident that she would never be in their position. But the Guyana of 1979 was much changed. The people she had known well, many of whom she had helped, were mostly all gone, passing like ghosts, gliding north across the Atlantic to become professionals serving others who already, she felt, had a surfeit of medical advantages. The country was now in the hands of self-important men in 'shirt jacks' who called each other (and you) 'comrade'; carried leather briefcases; drank brandy at the Pegasus; and glided through the city on the wheels of sleek Mitsubishis. Bombastic men, and sometimes women, who talked of "making the poor man the real man," while privately making arrangements for their own emigration.

Stalked by illnesses of age, Eunice's friends, the young men and women she had come of age with on the West Coast of the Demerara, were dying. Reading the *Sunday Chronicle's* "In Memoriam" columns now unsettled her. ...Five years have passed since that sad day/ When our dear Hilda was called away./ Few can know and only some can tell/ The pain of parting without farewell... Sometimes she wondered uneasily who would write *her* memorial. A northeaster gently played among the freshly cut roses in the gallery, its floor gleaming darkly with Mansion polish, hibiscuses and bougainvillea standing elegantly in a large vase on the plant stand in the drawing room. The deep sweet smell of all these flowers, floating in and around the highly varnished mahogany furniture, reminded her of Woo Ming's Funeral Parlor on a hot Sunday afternoon. She shivered in the Berbice chair, then shrilly called the yard boy and ordered him to "run quick-quick, run guh call Sister 'Gatha."

When 'Gatha got the message, she sensed that all was not well. Eunice had never sent for her on a Sunday afternoon. This was the time when 'Gatha and Leon would take the children for a drive on the "seawalls." They would leave Kitty, sometimes taking neighbors' children along with their own, and the battered Morris Minor taxi, its back weighted down by the children in the back seat, would crawl protestingly on its way up the Seawall Road to the Roundhouse near Fort Groyne. Taking the portable radio, they would all walk out on the long stone wall jutting out into the Atlantic that seemed a mystically thrashing, lashing thing with an awesome, hypnotic life of its own. They would watch the waves, feel the wet spray, inhale the smell of fish full in their faces, and see an occasional shark's fin rise briefly in the water. Often there would be lovers at the Groyne, their bodies close, their occasional silences punctuated by whispers.

'Gatha would watch them enviously, trying to be grateful for Leon's gentleness, but sometimes longingly recalling the roughness of Eustace's touch, the warm, husky urgency of his voice in lovemaking, the smooth sureness of his hands as they moved over her body, molding her passion to his in a frenzy of ecstasy. She would tear herself from the memory and try to focus on the children, holding the smaller ones close and warning the others of the licking they would get when they returned home if they played too near the edge of the wall. But Eustace was always there, his face overshadowing Leon's, his dead spirit in the Atlantic waves beating mercilessly against the Groyne like it did the unrequited passion that she still felt for him.

Sometimes 'Gatha cursed herself for being unable to love Leon in the same way as she had Eustace. After all, what the hell was wrong with her? If he could, Leon would have given her and the children (including Eustace's) anything they wanted. Leon whose great heart and large hands were always open to them all. As he began to show an interest in her after Eustace's death, she thought that she could grow to love him.

When he had first approached her, she was a passenger on the Kitty/Regent bus he was driving and she was in *puckaterry*, a virtual poster gyurl for post-traumatic stress. In a panic at being left without any prospect of paternal support for her remaining children and feeling that it was now she one and God, she had gone to the Police Headquarters at Brickdam to plead with Eustace's superior, Police Superintendent Nelson Irving, for financial help. True, in terms of their own relationship, she had decided to leave Eustace *at the foot of the cross*, but after his death, she felt that she owed it to his children to try to get them aid through the government employees' "Widows and Orphans" Fund. Superintendent Irving had made it clear to her that the government made no financial provision for the "illegitimate issue" of deceased police officers. Furthermore, the fact that Eustace, a policeman, had committed suicide after stabbing a woman to death only steeled Irving against bending any rules in favor of Eustace's children.

As 'Gatha disconsolately joined the Kitty-Regent for the trip back to Kitty, she would have confessed her love to the devil himself if he had shown her the slightest kindness. If *ole people seh, "Hungry dag ah nyam kyalabash,"* Leon Benjamin, the bus driver, became the calabash that caught her draining spirit—at least for the time being.

Now they were both in a situation which threatened them and their children and 'Gatha would take help from anywhere.

Eunice's call would prove the old Creole saying that *"God doan come, but 'e does sen'"*

It was a hot afternoon late in July 1979 when 'Gatha ascended the long back steps of Eunice's house on High Street. Eunice had never objected to her using the front steps, but knowing her as she did, 'Gatha felt that it would be presumptuous to do so without an invitation. After admitting 'Gatha, Doreen, the maid went to the drawing room to let Eunice know, "Yuh 'ave a visitor mam." 'Gatha and Doreen exchanged knowing looks as the latter ushered her into Eunice's presence. Doreen lived in Barr Street in Kitty and had become friends with 'Gatha at the Kitty Methodist School. They had remained close friends throughout their growing up and Doreen had been a source of comfort to 'Gatha during her troubles with Eustace. She had encouraged 'Gatha's subsequent relationship with Leon and was Precious and Princess' godmother. Doreen had worked for Eunice since she (Doreen) had taken and failed her school-leaving examination, and when Eunice told her that she needed a new seamstress, Doreen had immediately recommended 'Gatha.

Eunice sat reclining languidly in the Berbice chair, a large straw fan in one hand. The sounds of the Police Male Voice Choir singing *"Ave Maria"* gave way to those of the hymn, "A Mighty Fortress is Our God," sung by a mass choir and emanating from the large old Philips radio at her right hand. A fine dewy film of perspiration lay on her forehead. It was one of those hot, still, humid Guyana days when you could almost touch the moisture in the air.

With the straw fan, Eunice waved 'Gatha to a seat in one of the Morris chairs. 'Gatha's eyes swept the room. The spacious drawing room and formal dining room by themselves were probably almost the size of her family's cottage. The grand piano intrigued her because she had never heard it played, and she always dreamed of having Precious and Princess take piano lessons and of their being able to play for the admiration of the villagers at the St. James-the-Less Concerts. Sometimes she imagined Precious and Princess being courted in a drawing room like this by young men who would hold them in high esteem. She imagined such young men visiting them at this spacious house in Kingston with its long gallery and many expensive tropical plants, their leaves moving languidly in the north-easterly breeze. She saw these young men *writing home* to Leon for their hands in marriage. This house through which passed the subdued murmurs of servants' lowered voices and the occasional rush of ocean breeze punctuated by ominous silences would have been one of laughter for her family had they lived there. How would she ever be able to afford this for her children?

"How you do, gyurl? How di fam'ly dem?" Eunice asked. Eunice always condescended to use Creolese when dealing with her employees.

"Deh alright. Deh goin' *kitta katta*," 'Gatha replied. She thought that she would keep short her replies to such inquiries in order to help Eunice get quickly to the point.

"I saw Dr. Veerasammy again yesterday," Eunice sighed. "He tell me that he thinks I have cancer."

This news, delivered so matter-of-factly, jolted 'Gatha.

"Oh God!" 'Gatha exclaimed softly with a quick intake of breath as the tears sprang to her eyes. "A sorry. A *so* sorry, Miss Eunice."

In spite of Eunice's brusque demeanor, 'Gatha had grown to admire, the older woman. After all, how many other women had been able to achieve materially what she had? In this country, all the cards were stacked against women. You had to join the ruling party's women's arm or have a party card to ensure that you got so many necessities. Every night you went to sleep anxiously doing mental arithmetic to determine the cost of feeding your family for the week. You prayed that the taxi's engine parts would hold up, that the bald tires would be forgiving. That the old Necchi sewing machine would remain faithful to your touch. That the children, particularly the younger ones, Precious and Princess, would not catch the dangerous mosquito-borne Dengue Fever. That when they caught *any* fever or cold, the lemongrass tea that she brewed and eucalyptus oil that she sprinkled on their pillows would work to make them better. That the mosquito net would take some more darning so that they would be protected from these annoying insects and the diseases they carried. Forget the doctors. Even if you had money, you had to wait too long to see one, and when you did they were invariably overworked and underpaid.

But here was a woman who had money, and it seemed that she too might be in *puckaterry*.

Outside on High Street, a car horn sounded; the radio choir moved smoothly into "How Great Thou Art," the lilting sounds reinforced by those from the radio in the home of the Government Permanent Secretary across the street. Holding hands and swinging them, two young girls rode by, carefree on their bicycles, their laughter ringing shrilly through the street as they pedaled their way up to the seawall. For the rest of her life, 'Gatha would remember with absolute clarity the sights and sounds of these moments immediately after Eunice gave her the news.

"I've decided to seek another medical opinion in the United States. I need someone to accompany and assis' me in personal things. You are the best person I could think of."

Eunice paused here, seeming slightly out of breath.

"I will write my God-daughter, Celeste, in Brooklyn to fine out if we can both stay with her. She works in radiology at a hospital there an' I'll ask her to make de necessary arrangements. Of course, I would make sure that you're well paid, and I will take care of your travel and accommodation. After my treatment is finished, we'll come back immediately. Dese blasted doctors here doan know *what* deh talkin' 'bout."

It appeared that she had taken it for granted that 'Gatha would jump at the opportunity to go to the States. Indeed

'Gatha was thrilled to go, but thoughts of the children and Leon took the edge off her enthusiasm. How would they manage without her? Yet they needed the extra money. Eunice seemed a little surprised when 'Gatha told her that she had to go home and talk it over with Leon, but she said nothing. They talked some more and then 'Gatha rose to go. As she opened the door leading from the drawing room into the formal dining room, she heard a sudden furtive rustle behind the door as Doreen who had been eavesdropping there jumped back quickly and pretended to be clearing a nearby cupboard. She smiled nervously at 'Gatha and preceded her out through the dining room past the pantry and into the kitchen.

"Suh is whuh she seh?" Doreen whispered in inquiry once they were in the kitchen.

"I doan know. *You* tell me. Yuh mussie hear all uh it by now."

Doreen giggled softly, but 'Gatha was serious.

"Why yuh tekkin' people misery an' mekkin it laugh, gyurl? Eh! Eh! *Whuh is joke fuh small boy is det fuh crapaud.*"

Doreen sucked her teeth and ignored this. Sometimes 'Gatha could be too damn contrary. Over the years, after having suffered numerable slights in Eunice's employ, Doreen was often equivocal in her feelings towards her employer.

"Suh yuh goin'?" Doreen asked conspiratorially after recovering herself and feigning a more sober demeanor. "Better question. When yuh guh, yuh comin' back? Yuh would be a fool not to tek advantage of a opportunity like dis. Yuh know how many people dyin' to *defeck* an' get pun a plane out uh dis place?"

"Look, stop askin' me meh business," 'Gatha said, steupsing her teeth and stomping down the back steps. "A will talk to you before Evensong." Both women tidied the pews in St. James-the-less before the evening service.

'Gatha was angry that Doreen had eavesdropped on Eunice's request and that, *on the back of it,* she seemed unsympathetic to her employer's plight. But 'Gatha was even more furious that Doreen had verbalized the feeling, not yet even a formed thought, that flitted around the edges of her own consciousness— that she, 'Gatha, would seize this opportunity and not return with Eunice. After all, anyone with a grain of sense understood that when one person knew something it was a secret; more than one and it was print for the *spit press.*

'Gatha went out into the oven-like heat of Barrack Street where Leon waited then settled into the tattered upholstery of the taxi's front seat. As Leon pulled away, she missed the exchange of meaningful glances that passed between him and Doreen who stood at the foot of the back steps.

CHAPTER THREE

That night 'Gatha and Leon lay in bed and talked about the prospect of her going to America. Of course, she mus' go, he said. She mus' go if she wanted to an' t'ought it would help. He suggested that since Precious and Princess were so comfortable with their Nennen, Doreen, she might be asked to help care for them in the three or four weeks in which Eunice projected that she and 'Gatha would be gone.

"Yes, gyurl," he said, his rough hand stroking her face. "Go an' see whuh de place is like. Go an' have de experience fuh me an' de chirrun dem. Afta rall, none uh we family evah bin away before. We gun be okay till yuh come back. Doan forget to look up Evadne."

The night before she departed from Lamaha Street, one would have thought that she was leaving for good. Miss Ada and Miss Edna, two elderly village women who sold black pudding, came to bid her good bye and bring sugar cake, guava cheese and other confections for her and their sister, Miss Ida, who had migrated to Brooklyn years before when her son sponsored her.

"Heh, gyurl," Miss Edna said, pressing the package into her hands. "Walk wid dis. Tell Ida we miss she an' we sen' we love an' we blessin's."

Miss Joycie, Mama Rose and Doreen were also there. Doreen had agreed to help with housekeeping while she was gone. Two of 'Gatha's village clients sat in the dining area listening to *The Tides of Susanburg*, a local radio soap opera. Her young teenage sons hovered around her apprehensively. Leon and his lodge brothers were sitting around a table under the cottage, drinking *X-M Rum* and ginger ale and eating black Pudding and souse while Precious and Princess played hopscotch in the yard with their friends.

The women spoke of her impending departure and, though no one in the group had ever been there, what she should expect in Brooklyn. They all knew someone who had "bin up North" and fancied themselves second-hand experts on the place. No one made any reference to her return. Her two clients had *child fathers* in Brooklyn who had not seen, contacted, or supported their children in years. Instructing 'Gatha to get in touch with them in Bedford-Stuyvesant, the clients brought photographs and letters from their children as well as these men's last known addresses. One client, Sheila, suspected that her *child father* might have left Brooklyn for "Connecteecut," but she urged 'Gatha to do what she could to locate him anyway. The Nennen of her friend Evadne came bringing a letter which she wanted 'Gatha to deliver to her.

The whole thing reminded her of the occasion when her friend and sewing partner, Gwennie Braithwaite had left for Canada years before. Then, she had never dreamed that she would have the same experience, never thought that she would have escaped from a situation in which for years after Eustace's death, she felt imprisoned. She looked around at the women in the room, poor but hard working, fearful of the future but God-believing, grim but always with hope for the future. Women for whom love and romance were luxuries poor women could not afford. Women who felt that men like Leon were like large, rough, but precious diamonds that one found only rarely in the Mazaruni gold fields. Women who thought that one of their kind would be lucky if all she got was a good provider who stayed with his wife and children and feared his God. Women who would consider her a trifling ingrate if they sniffed her discontent. Her eyes swept the circle of their faces and she observed in them and Leon her jailers; focused on her children and saw in them their hostages.

Father Collins came and blessed her. He asked God to take into his loving care their sister Agatha, to hold 'er in 'is hands as she crossed the ocean, to preserve 'er from the temptations of life in de bowel uh de beas', to keep her always pure an' free from sin. He cleared his throat before saying this last bit, feeling as he did that this admonition was always best directed at those he considered as being among the weaker sex.

The next morning Leon drove them all to the now re-named Timehri Airport to see her off. Eunice had decided that she would travel alone with her regular driver and meet 'Gatha there. Leon's taxi crawled through the heavy traffic in La Penitence, the hawkers, traders, donkey carts, dray carts, lorries, trucks, Velosolex bikes, autocycles, bicycles, pedestrians, and cars all making for a noisy melange. On the wall near the door, a small cake shop by the roadside displayed a sign that proclaimed boldly, "NO LIMERS ALLOWED."

The city gave way to country as they rolled along the East Bank Public Road. They passed through little villages with names like Houston, McDoom, Agricola, Eccles, Bagotstown, and Peters Hall. Occasionally catching sight of fruit vendors and barefoot children standing along the roadsides, 'Gatha felt her stomach lurch sickeningly as she considered the possibility that she might never see her own children or these sights again for some time. How would her children manage without her? What about Leon? Was he really expecting her to return? The Hindu temples at Providence and Herstelling came into view, and soon the sugar cane fields at Diamond, fertilized through the years with the blood, sweat and tears of sugar workers. Soon they were on the sweeping curve of the road at Grove, then watching the stunning, ethereal beauty of the sun reflected off the Demerara River at the tiny village of Good Success. After passing through Friendship, Garden of Eden, Relief, Supply, Land of Canaan, and Caledonia and Soesdyke, they finally came unto the rising, curving road leading to the Timehri Airport.

The Pan American flight would leave at one in the afternoon, heading to New York. Saying little, 'Gatha's boys hovered near as if to protect their mother from some impending, but indefinable doom. Eunice was already there in the departure lounge after they had checked in. When their flight was announced, 'Gatha hugged the children close. Precious and Princess began to wail.

"Nevah mine, nevah mine. Mommy *soon* come back, darlin'," she assured each one of them. "Mommy soon come back."

But they would not be consoled, and Leon had to peel them off her. He rose from his squatting position near the children to hold 'Gatha close, to whisper her name, and then Eunice was urging them to hurry because their boarding announcement had been called. *"The last and final boarding call..."* 'Gatha walked with Eunice out onto the tarmac, Eunice moving painfully and slowly. Glancing back over her shoulder, 'Gatha's her eyes searched for them in the "waving gallery." They were now lost to her, vanished in the mass of other people who had come to the airport to see their loved ones off. This Pan American plane that she had seen so often flying over Stabroek on its way north stood waiting on the tarmac, giant, metallic, impressive. She had never been this near to an aircraft before, let alone boarded one.

She helped Eunice up the metal steps, their footsteps clanging loudly along with the others. Glancing back occasionally, her heart pounded as the thought that she was leaving her children crystallized into reality. Her mental focus closed in on them; their faces and their sobs were uppermost in her mind with every faltering step that took her away from them. The realization slammed her that they and Leon were all she had.

The passengers settled in for the seven-hour flight to JFK. Tired by her preparations, her rising earlier than usual, and the trip from Georgetown to Timehri, and, most of all, her illness, Eunice slipped from mild irritability into a deep sleep. While she had taken a few local pleasure trips by air over the Kaieteur Falls and to Orinduik, she too had never traveled to the United States before. She was so preoccupied with her illness and its consequences that the whole novelty of the journey escaped her.

'Gatha got into conversation with an elderly East Indian woman across the aisle. Doing so helped to take her mind off the hollowness in her stomach, her tears for her babies, the urge to scream. The woman said that her "true-true" name was Rookmin but that she was known in her village of Meten-Meer-Zorg by her "fond" name of Dolly. This was also her first flight. As they exchanged information about their families, 'Gatha learned that Dolly was flying to join a son she had not seen in twenty years. He lived in Richmond Hill, Queens and had come to the United States at twenty. He had gotten a "lil hol' on" as a janitor in an apartment building where he shared an efficiency with a friend. Later he had become the "super," put himself through Queens College in Flushing and then graduated as an accountant. According to his mother, he had a flourishing business in Richmond Hill. Dolly related all this with pride tinged with sadness.

"Twenty year me nevah see am," she told 'Gatha. "Twenty year. Mi' wonda how 'e *stan'* now. Me wonda if 'e guh know mi'."

Her calloused hands were folded on her lap. Years of farm work had left her stooped and worn, but pride and hope struggled for a place on her countenance.

After a pause, she turned to 'Gatha and said, "But if me see am now, me would know am. Me *sure* me would know am," she said, sighed and laid her head back on the headrest.

'Gatha felt she could never endure such a long absence from her children. How did this woman bear it all those years?

The hustle and bustle of JFK left her paralyzed and befuddled.

"Hurry up, gyurl! Get the luggage! Doan stan' dare like a pillar uh salt." Eunice cried, tired and impatient. The journey had left her pale and exhausted. Passengers moved purposefully getting baggage carts and going through the usual airport entry requirements. Dolly too looked bewildered by it all. When they got out into the taxi area, 'Gatha saw her approach two young men who had come to meet their relatives. By their accents, 'Gatha recognized them as Guyanese.

"You see wan Indian man out hay? 'E a drive wan red kyar," Dolly ventured hesitantly.

They looked at her, sniggered, and one of them said loudly, "Na. Na. We na see am."

Then they all burst out laughing.

Celeste arrived having hastily left the hospital. She had requested a few hours off to pick them up at the airport. Tall and thin, she appeared to 'Gatha to be edgy and nervous. Eunice had helped to pay for Celeste's education, and she graduated from a New York college with a degree in radiology. As she drove them along Atlantic Avenue to her apartment in Park Slope, 'Gatha marveled at these new surroundings. What struck her most about New York was the litter and grime of the great city, but there was a strangely different smell and feel to the air, one that she would never be able to define in all the time she would live there.

In the two weeks that they spent at Celeste's apartment, they learned that Eunice's condition was too far gone for remedy. Doctors advised that as the cancer progressed, she should be kept comfortable. She might have about three to six months left to live. They were very matter of fact. I suppose when one does this very often, one begins to see people more as a homogeneous mass of suffering than as flesh and blood individuals.

'Gatha had made up her mind that she would remain in New York. It was not an easy decision. The faces of her children flashed in her dreams, their voices sounding constantly in her waking moments. The rough kindness of their father, his strong hands, his ready generosity and goodnaturedness— all tugged her back to the mudflat. Yet the memory of the years of want and uncertainty in Kitty, the constant, nagging fear that something terrible would happen to rip irrevocably the seams of their lives, her estimation of what she considered her children's tattered prospects if some effort were not made to improve their existence—all pushed her in the direction of staying. She felt that it made more sense to take a chance at finding work in New York than to return with Eunice and have the door to opportunity slam shut behind her— perhaps for good.

For the two weeks, she stayed with Eunice, endured her temper, cried with her, comforted her and made her as physically comfortable as she could until two days before they were scheduled to return home. She felt she owed that to her but said nothing to Eunice concerning her plan to abscond. The old lady had enough to deal with, she thought. In the meantime, 'Gatha called her friend, Evadne, telling her what she intended to do and asking if she could *beg a lodgin'* with her until she could get on her feet. Without hesitation, Evadne agreed. It was years since they had seen each other, and Evadne felt that 'Gatha would be good company. She gave 'Gatha directions on how to get to their apartment on Ocean Avenue, and on a Sunday morning, just before Celeste returned from her night shift, 'Gatha kissed the sleeping Eunice goodbye, (she had been heavily sedated), placed a letter to her on the dining table, and tearfully slipped out of the apartment with her small bag packed with all of her few belongings.

She had come to love the feisty, fearless woman who had taught her much about courage. She was grateful for the opportunity that Eunice had given her for what she considered a shot at a better life, but they could no longer continue on together if 'Gatha and her family were to do better. She knew Eunice well enough, realized that underneath her tough exterior, she loved 'Gatha and her family and that she would understand. As 'Gatha made her way down Sixth Street, she knew that she and Eunice would never see each other again. So that an approaching pedestrian would not see that she was crying, 'Gatha wiped away a tear and continued on to the Number 41 Bus Stop.

CHAPTER FOUR

I first met Evadne in mid-November 1963 when she re-placed 'Gatha's sewing partner, Gwennie Braithwaite, who left for Canada that month. Mrs. Braithwaite, Gwennie's mother had taught them all to sew. Evadne and 'Gatha worked well into the middle of the night, their laughter lilting as they recounted their experiences with men, the harshness of their lives, the naivete of their romantic expectations. While knowing in their hearts the shallowness of this prom-ise, they would vow ruefully, "Gyurl, never again. Never *nevuh* again." At the time that Evadne and 'Gatha started to sew together, I was getting ready to go overseas to study, and so I was somewhat distracted by my preparations.

Yet there were some impressions of Evadne that stayed with me. She was a tall, lithe young woman in her late teens, full of faith in the possibilities of the same life that had, so far, treated her indifferently at times and downrightly callously at others. She was possessed by a searching restlessness and a hunger to confide in anyone willing to listen to the voiceless scream of her pain. She told me that when she was four months old, her mother had died of malaria. However, 'Gatha privately relayed to me that the village *spitpress* reports indi-cated that Miss Gloria (Miss G, as she was familiarly known in the village) had died of tuberculosis at the Best Hospital "ovuh de river." Because of the social stigma attached to the illness, Evadne told people that Miss G had succumbed to malaria.

Miss G had earned a living by making local pastries and other food for sale to civil servants in some government offices in Georgetown. Evadne was the result of a discreet but brief sexual liaison between Miss G and a married Chief Accountant who worked in one of the offices in the Public Buildings. One month into the affair, the Chief Accountant abruptly terminated his association with Miss G and thereafter ignored her.

Ole people seh, "When man done suck cane, 'e dash peelin' pun grung."

Miss G never approached the Chief Accountant for child support, hoping that her silence on this score would signal to him her unwillingness to embarrass him, thereby leaving the way clear for him to privately satisfy his financial obligations. However, he continued to treat her like they were strangers. Four months later, a combination of *post partum* depression, insanitary living conditions, fatigue, poor nutrition, physical debilitation, and just plain emotional neglect all conspired in Miss G's succumbing to tuberculosis.

Upon being told of her death, the Chief Accountant was heard to remark self-righteously to a colleague in the lunchroom that while it was reported that Miss G had died of malaria, only God knows what sometimes killed such women. He then finished the phulourie that he bought from the new lunch lady whom he had been eyeing, "thip-thipped" his teeth clear of phulourie fragments, and returned to the administrative barricades upstairs to wrestle with the challenges of the government payroll.

At sixteen, Evadne discovered her father's identity. Neither the caution surrounding the illicit love affair nor its brevity had placed it outside the ambit of the village *spit-press*. Initially, like her mother, Evadne made no effort to contact her father. Earlier, her adoptive mother (in an effort to get Evadne off her hands) had told the Chief Accountant where Evadne lived, but he had not tried to get in touch with her. On a few occasions, she had seen him, his wife, and children passing in Alexander Street in his fancy two-toned light grey and beige Hillman Hunter sedan on their way up the East Coast. Evadne told me that when he passed, he had "kept his head straight." How, she wondered, could someone ignore the existence of his own child? How could his heart not long to reach out to the flesh of his flesh?

Once, Evadne had gone to the Our Lady of Fatima Church for the funeral of a friend's father. The deceased was the Chief Accountant's mechanic. She raised her eyes from her pew only to realize that seated directly in front of her were her own father and his wife. She felt the warm rage starting its low slow simmer in her gut, its taste bitter as bile in her mouth. She saw the round calabash-shaped birthmark on his neck, the same as her own birthmark that other children had teased her about when she was a child at the Kitty Methodist School. She keenly recalled the struggle to survive at the hands of hateful, abusive, distant relatives, felt the hands of adult males who groped at her childhood under the shadow of night when they thought that they would not be detected. Remembered the vilest human feeling of all—to be a child virtually devoid of adult love and protection. Bitterly sensed the relentless, punishing vibrations of a *Necchi*'s whirring that continued late into the nights. She fought to restrain herself from shouting from the pulpit that he was her father, the one who had knowingly left her defenseless. Then she heard the plaintive wail that rose and transformed itself into a shrill scream as her friend cried out for her own dead father, one who had acknowledged and loved her. As Evadne stared at the hard nape of her own father's neck, seemingly set against her, her heart grew dry and brittle. Near the pulpit, the Lady of Fatima stared out unseeing, from her alabaster eyes. As they were to the three children before whom she appeared, her arms were extended in support of her original message of hope and warning.

While Evadne and 'Gatha worked hard and made enough money to survive under ordinary circumstances, Evadne still found it difficult to make ends meet. She had a weakness for clothes and good times, a fondness which, when coupled with improvidence and uncertain income, spelled nagging penury. Often, she resorted to men friends to "top up" her finances and was known to be occasionally generous with her favors. It was at one of these times that she met and seemed to settle down with Burchell, a post man who had worked his way up from being a postal errand boy. Even though she sometimes gave him her time and favors, she never really took him seriously. After all, she thought, where was he going? Where could *he* take her? As far as she was concerned, he lacked ambition. After he "knocked off" at four o'clock, he sought his friends for noisy games of dominoes, sessions of aimless *tantalize,* and bouts with *Banks Beer.* Sometimes their Saturday nights were given to occasional jaunts to the city's nightspots—oh, and of course, he took her to the Bourda cricket ground when an international match was on. Burchell seemed to be perfectly content with his life as it was. Evadne was not—and could not see him as a long-term prospect, but for fear of losing his company, she never made him aware of her reflections.

One night, two weeks before Christmas in 1973, she was standing on Main Street after attending a wedding reception at the Park Hotel. She had gone alone because Burchell was visiting an ailing relative across the Demerara river. Years later when she reflected on it, she had to admit that she had looked her best that night; the strapless, deep cherry red satin and chiffon dress that she and 'Gatha had designed and sewn, clung to every alluring curve. The strappy, platform high heels set her long legs off to perfection. She was trying to get a 'short drop' taxi back to Kitty. It was a warm Demerara night; the branches of the trees lining Main Street rustled occasionally under the fingers of the cooling Atlantic breeze.

As she left the hotel, she noticed that an attractively dressed man who appeared to be in his late twenties had just missed a taxi which was pulling away from the curb. When he turned to open the door of the next approaching taxi, his hand closed over Evadne's, for she too had reached for the door.

She had to admit that he was fine looking, flush with manhood at its prime. Her eyes glided over his banlon shirt, its soft material clinging to the hardness of his back. He was tall and well muscled with a flat stomach that seemed to beckon her fingers, and his skin, Nugget brown, evoked images of hot, wet, moonlit cane fields waving through centuries. She was startled by her own quick intake of breath as she felt the warmth of his hand on hers. She thanked God that she had brought out the heavy artillery of that red satin and chiffon—as well as the *Charlie* perfume. It had all cost her nearly three weeks worth of sewing, and she prayed that her efforts would have been worth it.

They shared the taxi on the ride to Kitty, and along the way they got to know each other.

"I on mi' way to see some uh mi' ol' pardners in Plaisance," he said partly by way of introduction, settling himself into a corner of the seat and confidently extending his arm along its back.

"A believe deh expectin' a raise. You cyan' come home widdout somebody harassin' you fuh a 'top up'," he added ruefully.

"Dat is too true," she returned. "True-true. Somebody always got deh han' in yuh back pocket."

His name was Compton Thornhill, and he had spent the past five years in New York. He said that he worked as a 'security consultant' in the Empire State Building, and before migrating to New York, he had been an officer at the Georgetown Prisons. Having come home to pick up his residence papers from the United States Embassy, he was also visiting his mother and sisters who all lived in Hardina Street in the heart of the city. Their "throw back" cottage was full of his mother, his sisters, and his sisters' children, many of whom had come from the country to spend Christmas in town, and so he was staying at the Park. At first Evadne was sparing in giving information about herself—not so much because she did not trust him, but because he made her feel uncomfortably shy. She did, however, tell him her name—"Oh me? Ise Evadne. Evadne D'Olivieira"—and that she was a "Kitty gyurl."

"Lissen. It still early. Is jus' 8:30. Why we don' go up to de Starlight Café in Buxton? Dat is, unless you livin' home wid some *sweet man* who waitin' on you—or unless you got young baby."

He said this with his eyebrows slightly raised in an inquiring smile.

So far, he had done most of the talking. She figured that before opening up to him, she would get as much information as she could from him about himself. Of course, every woman wid a lick uh sense knew dat at times like dese, yuh *true* information would come not from him, but from dose who *knew* him.

"I doan have no sweet man, " she said demurely. "But what about yuh…*"pardners"*? Dey won' miss you?"

He knew what her emphasis meant and looked across at her and smiled.

"No, my… *"pardners"*… won't miss me," he returned, with more emphasis.

"Awright. We gun go to Buxton."

After all, what else had she to do but to go home alone? She thought that if he got fresh in Buxton, she would get word to, and solicit a rescue from, her mother's third cousin's husband, Dolphus, a Buxtonian and former national champion middle-weight boxer who ran a van service to and from the city.

"I live in Brooklyn off Eastern Parkway. Live dere fuh de pas' five years," he offered, sipping rum and coke and enjoying the warm velvet blackness of the Buxton night against the distant roar of the Atlantic.

She learned that after leaving the Prison Service, he worked as a deckhand on a ship that docked briefly in Georgetown. Later, when the ship arrived in New York, he disembarked for good. Her fingers moved around and up and down the cold glass of *Banks Beer*, and as the liquid warmed her inside, she felt unusually at peace with herself. Someone inside the Starlight Café had put on Harry Belafonte's "Mary's Boychild."

"*God*, I miss dese ole Chris'mas songs," he sighed, as Harry's velvety tones moved over and around the darkness. "Nutting like a good ole B.G. Chris'mas. I miss hearin' carols in the hot sunshine. You know dat right now in Brooklyn, dey are digging out from several inches of snow?"

He sighed, obviously enjoying her company. "What do you do for kicks in Kitty?"

He pronounced it like an American—"Kiddy."

"Oh me? Not much to know about me. I does sew. Ise a seamstress. I born an' grow in Kitty. Is really jus' me, me one an' God—an' mi good frien' 'Gatha."

She thought it prudent not to mention Burchell—at least not at this point.

"Some Saturday nights we does check out Belvedere to see if deh got a good ban'. 'Gatha an' me, we does sew together. My muddah dead since I was small small. A lil baby, yuh know? It hard, but in dis place yuh does have to try to make it. Yuh jus' have to trus' de man upstairs to see yuh t'rough."

Evadne felt a little hypocritical after she added this last bit. Abiding religious faith had never been her strong suit, especially at times when she felt most deserted and alone. She said this about "de man upstairs" because she thought that doing so would polish the image of herself that she was now crafting for him.

"How you does manage?" He asked. "Guyana is not easy fuh people who strugglin'. If yuh doan hustle, *kyat eat yuh dinna.*"

"A lot uh dese women hustlin' to keep a man by getting' baby. When I geh baby, I want to be Mistriz Whoever. Chirren need deh fadduh. Deh need a complete home."

He looked at her more closely. He was a little surprised by her observations. When he first met her, he did not feel that her thoughts went too far beyond her own attractiveness.

"But *you* don' look like you doin' too badly," he murmured teasingly, smiling gently, appreciatively eyeing the generous cleavage that the filmy dress offered.

In the background, local singer, Johnny Braff, purred the lyrics of his one-time hit, "It Burns Inside:"

Oh love is a thing that burns inside,
And you should never, *never* let it pass you by.
For it may never ever pass your way again.
So hold on to love, my friend...

Compton reached over for her hand and led her onto the small dance floor. They melted into each other, the music making their silhouetted forms one as they swayed to its rhythm. For a few minutes, Evadne forgot the pain of her father's desertion, the insistent, punishing whirr of the *Necchi* sewing machine, and the bleak drudgery of her days till now.

In the two weeks that Compton had left, he often visited her in the couple of cramped rooms she rented in half of a bottom flat of her *Nennen's* house in Alexander Street. The cheap plastic flowers on the rickety coffee table in the front room shook when the traffic rumbled past. The *rice-eaters* in nearby yards would start barking furiously when he came into the yard, and she loved to hear his low chortling laughter at them. Sometimes, arm in arm, they walked the old city at twilight, Compton soaking up the sights and sounds of Guyanese Christmases long missed. Once they stopped by an old jukebox parlour on Regent Street to listen to Lord Kitchener singing the Christmas calypso staple about Christmas in "da muddah country." One evening as they sat in the Roundhouse watching the full moon rise over the Atlantic, she told him her heart's secrets—her unrequited yearning for her father's acknowledgement, the desperate monotony of her days in the village, her intermittent feelings of hopelessness that life would not offer her anything more. Some evenings, they would walk along the sea-wall, not feeling the need to say much to each other, enjoying the cool kiss of the north-east trades and listening to the hum of traffic from the distant city. Occasionally, they would hear the sound of a dog's lonely bark from the Police headquarters at Eve Leary or, if they were near Fort Groyne, laughter and music from the Pegasus Hotel would waft towards them in waves across the dark.

On his last night in Georgetown, he took her to see his family in Hardina Street. Theirs was a small, crowded, noisy house made all the more so by the sounds coming from the abutting yards, the blaring traffic that seemed too close by. His mother was tiny and frazzled, distracted by the number of young grandchildren she helped to care for. His sisters eyed Evadne with faint, silent hostility. They suspected that she was the reason why they had not seen as much of their brother as they had expected, presumed that she might have received money from him that they felt was their due. Before leaving for the hotel, he hugged them all, gave his mother some money, which she immediately inserted in her bosom, and they all promised to come to the airport to see him off.

By the time that Compton was ready to leave for the Timehri Airport, he and Evadne were seriously attached, and she later told 'Gatha, *"Boat gone a falls."* On his last night, he promised Evadne that he would return for her. Afraid to question her good luck, Evadne did not inquire into the details, but crossed her fingers and tried to steel herself against the possibility of disappointment. There had been so much of it in her young life.

Then he asked her to keep herself only for him. *"Woman alone like kyalabash,"* he admonished, resorting to the old Creole saying. *"Ev'rybody wan pass an' dip dey han'."* It never occurred to Evadne to make the same request of him.

Immediately following Compton's departure, the heavy rains really set in that January. The loneliness settled over her like the pall of rain clouds over the coast until it seemed to her that even the sky was shedding its own tears in sympathy. Evadne's yard was flooded, and the water began to seep into her quarters on the lower flat. For days, it rained relentlessly, and one heard the angry clatter of raindrops on the zinc roofs in the yard. To make her situation even more miserable, she came down with a severe case of the 'flu, being also gripped by high fever, chills and a nagging cough. Her Nennen who lived in the upper flat brought down cooked meals and *nineted* her with *Vicks VapoRub.* Burchell and 'Gatha got her over-the-counter medications from the pharmacy at Barr and Alexander Street. For her, a doctor's services were an unthinkable luxury. In spite of her making it clear to Burchell that their affair was over, he came over as soon as 'Gatha told him that she was sick, and he seldom left her bedside. Three weeks after Compton left, just when she was feeling her worst, she got his letter.

As she tore open the envelope and read it, her hot, dry fingers shook from fever and expectation, and her parched lips silently formed the words she read, her red-rimmed eyes darting over the paper, her hair unkempt. If she agreed, he wrote, he would return in June when they would be married.

Evadne wondered if her fever had escalated into delirium. As a child with whooping cough, she had once lost days of cognition to delirium. Uninvited, 'Gatha snatched the letter from her and verified the contents. Evadne sank back into the rickety Simmons bed with a sigh of relief. 'Gatha's loud exclamations reached uptairs to Evadne's Nennen, engrossed in *The Tides of Susanburg*, and she called down to find out if Evadne's situation was getting worse. Not only had Evadne been able to snag a bridegroom, but she had secured one who would be able to wisk her off *de mudflat*, thousands of miles away from the stitch-by-miserable-stitch existence to which she had thought she was irrevocably wed.

Yes, maybe the man upstairs was *railly dare* and looking out for her. She saw herself shopping in the large New York department stores—as far as she was concerned, the closest earthly equivalent to heaven. All the fashions that she and 'Gatha had gazed at longingly in *Ebony* and *Essence*, fashions that they had awkwardly tried to replicate in their own sewing, would soon be within her grasp. Suddenly, Evadne began to cry, the dry, hoarse sobs wracking her frame. 'Gatha who could not be sure whether her tears were the result of illness or relief, hugged her, feeling her thin, hot body shivering with fever.

Following Evadne's recovery, she, 'Gatha and her Nennen began planning the wedding. Evadne yearned to have her nuptials officiated at St. George's Cathedral in the city where so many prominent people worshipped. She knew that her father and his family were regular communicants there, and she longed to tell him of the coming occasion, to have him escort her down the aisle in the presence of her bridegroom and her friends. Then all her friends would see that she did have family, that it was not just she one an' God. She could just see the picture in the *Sunday Chronicle* following the wedding, a photograph under the caption: "D'Oliviera-Thornhill Nuptials: Chief Accountant Gives Away Daughter in Cathedral Wedding." She kept her feelings to herself, never mentioning them to 'Gatha or her Nennen in whose eyes she thought she saw the shame and stigma of her father's rejection.

Some weeks before the wedding, without telling anyone, Evadne made her way to the Public Buildings. Over the years, her father was repeatedly promoted and now held another high government position. She had actually got to the precincts of the Public Buildings when her beating heart, queasy stomach, and cold, trembling hands made her feel that she was about to do something she would regret.

Wouldn't 'e t'ink 'er bare-face and *fawwud*? Wouldn't 'e t'ink dat she had taken God out 'er t'oughts? What de hell was wrong wid 'er? she asked herself.

She was seized by a strong desire to return to Stabroek Market and to flee on a minibus back to the refuge of her rooms in Kitty. But the primal human instinct for blood kinship proved stronger than that for self-preservation. She turned determinedly back to the Public Buildings and entered his carpeted outer office where she stood uncertainly, feeling that her cheap pale green cotton print dress made her somewhat out of place in the professional atmosphere where she now stood uncomfortably. Seeing her uncertainty and noting her discomfiture, his Senior Woman Secretary approached her. Fiftyish, this woman wore sensible heels and a tweedy-looking skirt, seemingly too warm for the tropics. The fans overhead creaked rhythmically as they briskly and indifferently moved the warm air and dust about. Evadne felt the sweat pouring down the back of her neck.

"Yeh-ess?" the woman inquired, peering over the rim of her glasses and, without appearing to do so, coolly taking in Evadne from head to toe.

She asked for Evadne's name and whether she had an appointment.

"No, I din make any appointment," Evadne said softly, now more self-conscious and uncertain than ever as two young smartly dressed female office workers drew unobtrusively near to hear the exchange, one pretending to be going through papers in a file jacket that she held, the other opening a nearby file cabinet, each occasionally glancing at Evadne.

Evadne did not know it then, but her father was so notorious for his illicit affairs that sometimes even the most innocuous visits of attractive women tended to excite mild curiosity in the office. He was now a top government official with enormous responsibility for the national finances but increasingly heedless of discretion in his personal life. The Senior Woman Secretary eyed her closely, seeming to recognize a resemblance between Evadne and her immediate supervisor.

"My name is Evadne D'Oliviera. I'm a relative." This a little more boldly from Evadne.

"Wait here," the woman said quietly and immediately turned to go into his office.

Through the open door, Evadne heard him say musingly, "D'Oliviera... D'Oliviera... I doan know any D'Oliviera."

Then between the two, there was a brief, murmured conversation in which the words were indiscernible.

The woman soon emerged with a dismissing "He says he doesn't know any D'Oliviera."

Evadne turned to go and was almost at the outer door when from within the inner office, she heard his impatient voice sighing loudly in second thought, "Awright, awright. Send 'er in, Mrs. Bacchus."

Years later in Brooklyn, Evadne recounted their meeting to me, the first time that she had done so to anyone. Her feelings were in tumult. As much as she wanted him to, she said that she almost regretted it when he agreed to see her. She fully expected that she would ultimately be dismissed from the office without being permitted to see him. She was prepared for that humiliation. In that case, she would not have to fault herself and would live with the knowledge that she *had* made the effort. Had he dismissed her immediately, what more could she have asked of herself? Now, however, more was expected of her. She was expecting more of him. Her heart beat so loudly that she was sure that Mrs. Bacchus and the two curiosity-seekers were hearing it.

She entered his office and was unprepared for the salt-and-pepper gray of his hair and his expanding waistline. It had been some years since she last saw him. He stood up as she came in and motioned her to a chair facing his desk. The office was neat and so was he, sitting under the ubiquitous picture of the Comrade Leader with the drooping eyelids and goatee, smiling benignly down from the wall like the picture of Jesus in her Nennen's house. She had no doubt that the man who now sat before her was her father. Nennen had always commented that Evadne "*favor* him bad, *too* bad." As much as she keenly sensed he was, Evadne herself was struck by their resemblance. He seemed somewhat taken aback, and his fingers trembled slightly when he raised his hand to his face to smooth his neat moustache.

"I'm Evadne," she said simply. "Gloria gyurl. Gloria D'Oliviera. Miss G." Funny how she couldn't bring herself to say, "I'm your daughter"—at least not yet.

"Who is Gloria D'Oliviera?"

He squirmed uncomfortably in his chair.

"She use to sell food in the Public Service in the fifties. I'm yuh daughter. She get me fuh you."

She added this awkwardly, stutteringly. She had rehearsed what she would say, but somehow it was all coming undone.

"Mi' mother died soon after I was born, an' deh tell me dat you are my fadduh."

"Look gyurl," he said, rising and sighing heavily. His hands shook. "I t'ink you wastin' my time. You mus' be mixing me up wid somebody else. I have *two* daughters dat I know of—an' dat's it."

Actually, as he later told one of his friends at the Palm Court where he had a gin and tonic that night, he was stunned by Evadne's resemblance to his older daughter, Claire. The difference between the two young women was that while Evadne appeared jaded and tawdry, Claire was gently reared and showed it. She and her sister, Michele, attended the best girls' school in the country, were classical pianists interested in the ballet and in art, were both brilliant students who planned to study medicine overseas. Claire planned to specialize in pediatrics and Michele in gynecology. He could not have been prouder. Indeed, their accomplishments eased his initial disappointment that he had no sons.

"But I *know* dat you's my fadduh," Evadne protested, trying not to cry.

"I'm gettin' married soon, an' I would like you to kerry me to church."

In the silence that followed, Evadne heard the clackety-clack of typewriters loud in the outer office. The softly whirring upright fan in the corner of his office turned from side to side as if in slow negation.

"Look. I remember Gloria now."

He said this in a lower tone, confidentially and slowly as though with dawning recognition. "But she an' I never got close enough for me to get her pregnant. She was a nice gyurl an' it is good to see that her daughter is getting' married, but I am not your father, chile. You kyan jus' walk off di' road an' come in here an tell me I am yuh fadduh an' you want me to carry you to church. I am not yuh fadduh, gyurl!"

As he said this, his eyes darted furtively towards his office door which was slightly ajar. He got up and moved to close it just as the Senior Woman Secretary guiltily jumped away from the filing cabinet close by.

"Heh. Take dis money an' I hope it helps with your wedding, but I'm certainly not the person to be carrying you to church."

His tone implied that the conversation was over.

He reached into his pocket, withdrew some notes from his

wallet, and extended them towards her, his hand shaking slightly.

Evadne's eyes filled with tears. She rose and walked slowly past his outstretched hand. She drew herself up to her full height, lifted her chin and looked at him levelly. As she turned to go, he noticed the calabash birthmark on her neck, just like Claire's—just like his.

Suddenly, no longer tongue-tied, she said with a newly found vehement strength, "I *never* di' want yuh money. I *only* di' want mi' fadduh."

She walked past the Senior Woman Secretary and the two Class II clerks in the outer office into the fresh air on Brickdam. It was the first time that she had not accepted a gift from a man.

Some weeks later, Compton returned and in the middle of the June rains, he and Evadne were married at St. James-the-Less Church in David Street. There was no need for 'Gatha and Evadne to make the wedding dress because Compton said that he had a relative in the Flatbush area who he thought was Evadne's size, and she chose (and tried on) a dreamy beaded lace and tulle creation from a Brooklyn store. It fit Evadne like a glove and 'Gatha said that as Evadne walked down the aisle on the arm of the Buxtonian and former prize-fighter, Dolphus, she looked "out of dis worl' gyurl. Out of dis worl.' " The few relatives in the church fanned themselves, as perspiration seeped slowly from under their tightly pressed curls. The organ's strains of "Blessed Be the Tie that Binds" provided a doleful backdrop to 'Gatha's memories of the jilting Eustace, now lost to suicide, her recollection of the stillbirth she had undergone, all returning as a painful reminder as she glanced out from the wedding to his grave in the churchyard. She did not wish to rain on Evadne's parade but she silently wondered how well Evadne knew Compton and whether he would "always show her a true face." Afta rall, she jus' meet de man, and sudden sudden deh get married.

At the house of Evadne's Nennen, they had a small reception catered by Miss Ada and Miss Edna and at which Compton's mother unconvincingly expressed the certainty that she was not losing a son but gaining a daughter. His sisters remained sullen. Compton made the bridegroom's speech with its obligatory first mention of "my wife and I" at which the guests laughed dutifully.

Two days later, Compton returned to Brooklyn. He would "put in" Evadne's papers and send for her later. Months later, Evadne left Guyana for married life in Brooklyn. 'Gatha, her Nennen, and the black pudding ladies, Miss Ada and Miss Edna, saw her off at Timehri airport. Ada and Edna had tucked sugar cake and two Buxton spice mangos into her luggage (one for Evadne and the other for their sister, Miss Ida, who had emigrated some years before and now lived with her son in Bed Stuy). Evadne moved into a two-bedroom apartment on Cortelyou in Brooklyn which she and Compton shared with his mother's sister and other relatives.

By this time, I had already left Guyana, but 'Gatha had written one of her few letters to me that Christmas of 1973, a letter enclosed in a Christmas card depicting a snowy scene complete with sled and woolen clad skaters. In it, she kept me apprised of her thoughts about the wedding. In spite of her initial elation, to 'Gatha, the whole thing now seemed a little too *hurry-up hurry-up*. But who was she to tell her friend this? Having been jilted years earlier, 'Gatha did not want to seem to throw cold water on Evadne's happiness, to appear envious, or what was even more the case, I suspect, to reveal the crack in her calabash that Evadne's eventual departure for New York would force. She could not help asking herself (and Leon who was becoming mildly irritated by her questions) what Evadne know 'bout dis man, dis knight in a banlon shirt and well creased pants, dis knight who ride in on a jetliner. When I got her letter, I wondered what kind of person

Compton was in cramped conditions in the sub-zero snows of a New York winter or the oven-like temperatures of its summers? Would he be patient with Evadne? Soothe her when she was low? Temper her restlessness and hurt when the demons of her early life banged on their door? Would their love persist through their lives as part of the world's forgotten human detritus, now strangers washed up on an alien shore?

Evadne had written 'Gatha glowing letters about Brooklyn, telling of the great life to be had in New York, speaking of Times Square, Broadway, the Twin Towers, the Empire State Building and other landmarks as though they were part of a glamorous everyday life she led. In reality, however, in the years that followed, she worked long, oppressive hours in Manhattan's garment district, waking early in all weathers to take her child to a baby-sitter and to be in time to catch the subway to work. She returned exhausted late in the evening for three days a week; she sometimes worked as a housekeeper for a Jewish woman in the East sixties. Compton was a security guard at the Empire State building working nights and on weekends helped a friend to refurbish basements in East New York.

Six years later, when 'Gatha knocked on the door of their two-bedroom Ocean Avenue apartment, she and Evadne would meet again. From inside, she could hear the cries of a small child. It was Sunday, Evadne's only day off, and she was cooking split pea soup, just like she and 'Gatha would have done in Kitty six years before when they were both single and had some free time on a Sunday. Evadne had just pealed the plantains she had bought from a Korean green grocer off Eastern Parkway, and since she had no mortar and pestle, she would grind the boiled plantains in the blender to make *fufu*. Yuh had to make de bes' uh t'ings. The apartment was steamy with the smell of onion, garlic, fine leaf thyme, and pigtails.

Evadne opened the door, and they hugged each other and screamed with the joy of meeting. They had missed each other sorely. In the midst of their greeting, they paused to take each other in. Evadne had filled out physically and still seemed to have some of her old spirit, but an older, more serious cast lay about her eyes. The difficulties of survival in New York were beginning to take their toll. She took hold of 'Gatha's arm, drawing her further into the hot, crammed apartment. Evadne's five-year old daughter stood by the bedroom door, her tear-streaked face peering around the door to get a better look at their visitor. Remembering Precious and Princess, 'Gatha smiled at the child and reached down to touch her damp cheek.

"Eh! Eh! Well how yuh do nuh gyurl?" Evadne asked. "How yuh do? Eh! Eh! It look like you put on a little."

Evadne said this looking up and down the length of 'Gatha. Before 'Gatha could reply, she added, "But is better dan lookin' *mawga*."

"Well you got a nerve, gyurl," 'Gatha exclaimed. "You en look too *mawga* yuhself."

They both laughed and little Hope smiled, looking from one to the other of them.

Sappodilla-brown, Evadne was physically well built, (*hellty* in Guyanese parlance), having about her an air of restlessness. Again, she opened her arms wide and hugged 'Gatha long. The smell of split peas soup filled the apartment, and Hope who bore a striking resemblance to her mother, soon sat on 'Gatha's lap. 'Gatha felt more at home, slowly losing the weepy, homesick feeling for her family that she had carried with her since she arrived in New York. 'Gatha began to relax, listening to her prattle on, her tones evoking the East Coast of the Demerara and hinting at strong, warm sea breezes rustling through the coconut tree branches.

"Suh how de gyurls dem? How Precious and Princiss?" Evadne asked.

"De smell uh dat soup remine me *so* much of dem." Here, 'Gatha's voice broke a little. "Deh goin' aright. A lil asthma hare an' dare, but deh tryin'." She did not want to go right away into their difficulties at home.

When Evadne left, Precious and Princess had not yet been born, but later, every Christmas, she would send them clothing and other necessities.

"How dem boys? How Leon? Eh! Eh! How Nennen? Wha' 'bout Miss Ada and Miss Edna?" Evadne asked, feeling that if she kept talking, she would distract 'Gatha from the pangs of missing she knew that her friend was suffering.

Evadne who had known 'Gatha since childhood when they played "Wedding Cake, Stale Cake" and "Littie" and "Hopscotch" in the school yard long after almost everyone had gone knew her friend well. The passage of the years and their reduced association had not diminished their mutual understanding. After Eustace left 'Gatha who struggled with depression that almost took her life, Evadne had been there caring for 'Gatha's boys, one of whom was her godson, forcing on 'Gatha the same kind of soup that now bubbled on the stove.

"Oh Goy!" 'Gatha exclaimed. "Yuh have to gi' me time to answer all dese questions. Yuh Nennen sen' dis letter fuh you. Everybody well an' hope dat you livin' in de Lord's love, gyurl.   What about Compton? Is how 'e do? Is wheh 'e deh?"

CHAPTER FIVE

As they settled around the dining table, Evadne and 'Gatha chatted for a while about everyday matters, then Evadne brought her up to date about her life so far in the United States. Initially, she and Compton settled in an apartment on Cortelyou where he had been living with his aunt who, like her sister back in Hardina Street, had a crowded home. (Evadne understood more clearly now why Compton would have wanted the peace of the Park Hotel in Georgetown). He explained the fact that he was still living at his aunt by saying that it was cheaper for him to do so when he was single. He did not tell Evadne this, but before she came to New York, he had spent most of his time at the home of his girlfriend *du jour*, using his aunt's apartment as a kind of refueling station. During the day, his aunt took care of four grandchildren between the ages of about four and nine. Two of her own teenage children also lived there, as well as a middle-aged female relative who worked four days a week as a live-in in Jersey and, on the other three, slept on the living room couch. From the babysitting and the rent that she collected from Compton and the couch-dweller, as well as additional "top ups" that she received from her grown children, (Compton's cousins), his aunt was able to keep body and soul together.

Even though she herself had not hitherto enjoyed splendid living conditions in her shabby little Kitty bottom half, there, Evadne had at least the luxury of privacy and control over her immediate surroundings. After nine o'clock in the evening, the silence descended on the village, and one could *hear* one's thoughts. In her present cramped New York conditions, she found herself stressed and exhausted by the proximity of strangers whose loud conversations and laughter, snoring, belching and bathroom sounds made her uncomfortable and nervous on the nights when she was alone, waiting for Compton to get home from work. The situation painfully recalled her orphaned childhood and adolescence growing up among intolerant and abusive strangers. Compton could not understand her responses, and one night he whispered angrily (and with surprising vehemence) to her that she was being "an ungrateful lil bitch." Afta rall, he said, at home she had given him the impression that she would have been thrilled just to be in New York. She felt chastened by his comment and vowed to keep her thoughts about their living conditions to herself from then on. As Evadne continued with her story, the pressure cooker in the kitchen startled them with the blast of its whistle, and Evadne got up to check it while she continued.

The blare and rumble of traffic and constancy of police sirens proved New York to be truly the city that never slept. Even at two in the morning, they could hear footsteps on the street or people talking to each other—often drunks arguing, or drunks being "rolled." The littered sidewalk, garbage cans that often overflowed, all these conditions conspired to make her disappointment and depression profound.

When she had first arrived in New York, Compton told her that as soon as she found a job, they would be able to relocate. She immediately began going through the ads in the *Daily News* and *New York Post* and after lying to a housekeeping agency about her past experience, soon found a job working for an elderly couple, the Steins, on the upper East Side. He was a retired Manhattan jewelry dealer and she was a mother and housewife. They were a kindly couple, but harboring dreams of eventually starting her own dressmaking business, Evadne had no interest in cleaning other people's homes and merely wanted to earn some money. One day, in the midst of scrubbing the kitchen floor, she intimated her yearning to Mrs. Stein who after a year, introduced her to relatives who owned a dressmaking business in the fashion and garment district. Evadne was soon working there part time in addition to working for the Steins. Having entered the United States as European refugees after the Second World War, they understood what it meant to be strangers on the shore, and something in Evadne's demeanor evoked their compassion.

After a few months, Evadne was beginning to think that Compton had no intention of moving from his aunt's place. Regretfully, she was coming to the realization that her decision to marry him was too hurried, that she had needed to know more about him. What was it Miss Edna had said to her so many times? What was it? Oh yes! "Marry in haste; repent at leisure! Watch wheh yuh steppin' gyurl! Watch wheh yuh steppin'! " When they had met in Georgetown, she had the impression that he was much more independent than he now behaved. At first the excuse he gave for not wanting to move was that she needed to find a job so that they would have more money coming in. When she secured two jobs, his next explanation was that they needed to save more money. He never said it outright, but she had the impression that even though he himself took no precautions against the eventuality, he would not have been thrilled if she became pregnant.

Evadne was growing tired of the living conditions in Cortelyou, of having to lower her voice when she and Compton argued, of needing to whisper when they made love, of smothering their giggles over the snoring of the Jersey live-in. His aunt resented displays of affection between them, and she treated Evadne more as an unwelcome girlfriend than as his wife. Secretly, his aunt felt that Compton would have been much better off marrying a Harlem girl whom he had been seeing for a few years before he met Evadne. To her chagrin and irritation, Evadne noticed that Compton stopped showing her any affection when they were around his relatives.

Evadne hated having to listen to her in-laws' children yelling day in and day out. She wanted her own—and space in which to rear them. In the six months that they lived there, Compton spent much time away from the apartment, offering work as an excuse to escape Evadne's growing complaints and the apartment's noise. Even as she complained, Evadne felt guilty because he said that he worked overtime so that they could save faster. Often, when she was not working, Evadne was left alone in the company of these people whom she did not know, and whom, under ordinary circumstances, she would not have cared to. She regarded them as coarse folks, possessed of free-floating hostility, who answered the phone with " 'oo dat?" Once when Mrs. Stein needed her to work in an emergency situation, she almost lost the day's pay because Mrs. Stein could not believe that she had gotten the right number and was on the verge of hanging up after calling back.

Matters came to a head in the middle of the morning one Saturday when, unusually, Evadne was home alone. Compton's aunt was a Jehovah's Witness, and she, the children and grandchildren were out delivering The Message.

There was a knock at the door and when Evadne opened it, standing outside was a pregnant woman of about her own age.

"Yes?" Evadne inquired. "Can I help you?"

As soon as Evadne saw this woman who looked so much like her in stature, features and age, uneasiness crept over her. She felt it in every pore like the beginnings of malaria chills in the middle of the rainy season on the Demerara foreshore. Why de hell she knockin' on *dis* door? Evadne wondered, hoping that the woman was trying to find some other tenants in the building. The names were always falling off the mailbox in the shabby lower lobby, and sometimes people knocked at their door to inquire about the whereabouts of others.

Evadne's womanly instincts told her that there was about this woman a look of strangeness that hesitated right on the threshold of madness. Looking into her eyes, Evadne felt that she stared into the frightening recesses of rage gone cold. If you had asked Evadne to explain it immediately afterwards, she said, she would not have been able to, but only years later, reflecting on her initial impressions, could she articulate it more clearly.

"I'm looking for Compton Thornhill," the woman said quietly—in an uptown New York accent, boldly, slowly, insolently, the corners of her mouth turned down ever so slightly in a mocking, quiet, faintly amused smile. She was dressed in a pale green fall coat with a collar of deeper green. She seemed to know who Evadne was, to sense her discomfiture, and to be enjoying herself.

"'E's not here," Evadne said. She felt somewhat diminished by this woman's well dressed assurance and apparent sense of entitlement and belonging, the way she had felt when she went to her father's office and spoke first to the Senior Woman Secretary.

Evadne's voice trembled *ever* so slightly, and her response was immediately followed by a tiny, nervous intake of breath. In this exchange where on both sides, human instincts were finely tuned, her discomfiture was not lost on the woman in green standing at the door.

Evadne's silence seemed an indication that she was not going to give any more information. Then she took hold of herself.

"I'm Mrs. Thornhill—his wife," she said firmly. " Cyan I help you?"

"Just tell him that Jennifer was here. Jennifer, *the mother of his child*," the woman stressed, patting the mound of her abdomen. Before Evadne could say more, she turned to go, then stopped at the top of the stairs where she paused and shot down the corridor in Evadne's direction, "I heard the wedding dress fit perfectly."

Evadne felt her mouth filling with saliva as a wave of nausea passed over her.

Then unhurriedly but purposefully, the woman started down the steps and left the building. Evadne's knees went weak. Mechanically, she closed the door, retreated into the apartment, and sank onto the sofa, clutching her stomach as though she had been sucker-punched. She spent the next few minutes in the apartment's one bathroom—retching.

CHAPTER SIX

Panicky, Evadne felt like one set adrift. Apart from Compton, Miss Ida (who lived in Bed Stuy and to whom she had spoken only three times by telephone in the nearly five months that she had been in Brooklyn) and the Steins, whose acquaintance she considered still distant, she knew no one else closely in New York. Her long working hours did not permit too much time for friendship and leisure. Had something like this occurred in Kitty, she could have talked to 'Gatha, her Nennen, and other women friends, all who might have given some bad advice but also a good deal of emotional support as well. When they thought she needed it, they were never shy about admonishing and chastising her verbally. When they presumed she required encouragement, they were always quick to surround and protect her. In many respects, they were the friends who mothered her when mother there was none.

If it turned out that what this Jennifer said was true, what could Evadne do? Could this stranger merely have been some demented mischief-maker who really had very little to do with her husband but who wanted to cause her suffering for no real reason? She doubted it. She was determined to get at the fire that lay at the bottom of this smoke. If what this woman was saying was true, where could Evadne, go? For the long, exhausting hours she worked, her earnings were pitifully small, and she still felt frightened, homesick and isolated in New York. As things stood, for the moment, her alternatives were painfully and severely limited. Compton was working a double-shift again and would not be home till the next day. He could not be contacted on his job so that she had much time to think about what she would say to him. Usually when he came in he was exhausted and not in the mood for conversation—far less confrontation. Waiting for him like this reminded her sorely of her apprehensiveness leading up to her approach to her father back in Georgetown.

She felt nauseous and so she dressed quickly and went out into the street to get some fresh air. There was a nip in the Fall day and birds were beginning to mass, preparing to leave the snow and cold to New Yorkers. She passed a woman with a small child who looked at her strangely, his little face smeared with chocolate, and his head hanging, swiveling back at her as they went by. She walked aimlessly for about an hour, then got on the "D" train for Prospect Park. She needed trees and open spaces to stop the feeling of strangulation that she feared would overwhelm her.

In spite of his tiredness, she tackled Compton the next day. Strangely enough, he was willing to discuss the incident. They left the apartment and walked together in silence so that they could talk away from the Cortelyou dwellers. They ended up in one of the Caribbean eateries in the Church Avenue area.

"So what do you want to know?" he asked.

"Who de *hell* is dis woman?" she demanded with spirit.

"I would appreciate it if you doan use dat tone wid me," he said. "I don't talk to *you* dat way."

Evadne was in no mood to be admonished. Here he was playin' *wrong an' strong* when she needed answers. She said nothing, distrustful of her ability to control herself and not to tell him to go straight to hell.

"Maybe you should hear my side firs' before yuh start flyin' off," he said evenly.

"I wonder if I cyan even *believe* anyt'ing you got to tell me," she returned, tearfully.

"Evadne, at leas' hear mi out! Hear mi' out!" He said this under his breath because other patrons were occasionally glancing curiously in their direction.

Evadne pushed aside her fury and listened.

Jennifer was a secretary in a company located in the Empire State Building where Compton worked as a security guard. They got to know each other because some nights she worked late and he saw her when he was scheduled for the third shift. After a while, they began dating and often he would stay over at her apartment on Convent Avenue in Harlem. They had been seeing each other for about three years when she began asking him about getting married. He was surprised because Jennifer always gave him the impression that she was quite independent and that she thought of marriage as constraining. Indeed, more than once, he had heard her say that marriage benefited men more than it did women. Her ideas suited him because they relieved him of any obligation he might have felt about "taking their relationship to another level" (as she had sweetly put it), and he was therefore lulled into a sense of complacency. After he got over his surprise, he told her that he felt that he was not yet ready even though at the time he was not seeing anyone else. Every day, her demands became shriller and more impatient. She accused him of using her to pass the time, and in spite of his protestations to the contrary, she never seemed to believe him. In reality, to him, Jennifer was like a "broken calabash"—used up. She had done her turn. He did not want to leave her, but he did not want to marry her either. His was a perplexing dilemma.

As well as for the purpose of securing his green card, the trip to Guyana afforded him a chance to clear his mind, to think the situation through without distraction. Then, his meeting Evadne proved to be a fortuitous turning point in the whole disturbing business. Evadne's emotional and material need called out to the *machismo* in him. He felt himself deeply attracted to the idea of a woman who not only desired but *needed* him as well—and showed it. Also, he was drawn to all Evadne embodied of home, the familiar, which he missed. Evadne had done her best to present herself to him as a woman, if not an ingénue, who had kept her own *kyalabash* intact. In all, I rather sense that as well as seeing marriage to Evadne as a personally felicitous event, he viewed it as a convenient means of disentangling himself from the relationship with Jennifer, one now going decidedly sour.

When he returned to New York, he made up his mind that he would tell Jennifer about his forthcoming marriage, but somehow he never seemed to have the nerve to broach the subject. Sometimes he would begin to tell her and she would cut him off to gush over some great outfit that she had picked up at Alexander's or Gimbel's or Macy's. At other times, she was just too tired to talk. About this time, her company was engaged in heavy auditing and inventory-taking and her hours were therefore longer.

On the matter of marriage, though, while her approach became somewhat more circuitous and her tone calculatedly less strident, Jennifer never dropped her demand that they get married. Furthermore, she resorted to disingenuous inducements that she imagined would change his mind. Once, in Brooklyn, they were passing a store on Ralph Avenue where she saw a "*gor*geous" bridal gown, and she urged him to go in with her so that she could try it on. She did and looked "faabulous" in it, "didn't he think?" He agreed and the next day, alone, he returned to the store and bought it. The fact that she and Evadne were just about the same size was not lost on him. What did escape him, however, was the old wives' tale of bad luck in having someone else try on a bride's gown before her wedding.

Just before he left to go back to Guyana for the wedding, he got up the courage to tell Jennifer that he had met someone whom he would return to marry. It was then amid her tears and rage that she told him that she was pregnant.

At first he thought that it was just a ruse that she had conjured up on the spur of the moment to deter him, but the disclosure jolted him nevertheless. How de hell could she be pregnant? The obvious answer lay in the successive nights of bare, passionate intimacy that consumed them after his return, nights when after each bout of love-making, he vowed that it would be the last—and after each one of these promises he would return.

According to him, when Evadne came to Brooklyn, he ended the relationship with Jennifer. However, he would still go to Convent Avenue to see how she was getting along. She was indeed pregnant and had no intention of "ditching my child" as she poutingly put it. He visited her often, giving financial support when necessary and even going with her to her doctor. However, he thought that her demands for money were becoming excessive and extravagant. His rejection of Jennifer's most recent requests for money, he felt, instigated her attempt to blackmail him with this visit to Evadne who now guessed that herein lay the reasons why they were marooned in his aunt's apartment and why he required that she work so much more. Evadne ground her teeth angrily.

As *he* explained it, the whole affair revealed him to have been unwittingly ensnared in a situation over which he had little control. What he said and how he related it made the whole matter one with which none but the unreasonable and intolerant would quarrel.

"Leh me tell you *dis*, Compton!" she said hotly under her breath so that the other patrons would not hear, but leaving him no doubt about how angry she was.

"De firs' ting is dat by de en' uh dis mont', we gettin' out uh dis woman place. After den, I am not livin' anodduh day—not anodduh *secon'*—unduh anoddah woman roof. *Two big 'oman kyan live in de same house,"* she said, citing the old Creole proverb. "Even in Kitty, I had mi' own roof."

"De nex t'ing is—dis presumptuous wretch who because uh you, *tek she eye an' pass me!* Tek God out she t'oughts an' come to distress me? Look at my crosses! You gun finish it wid she because I doan believe dat you an' she done! I doan give a fart dat she getting baby fuh you! How de *hell* you know is you own?"

Compton said nothing for a while, thinking it best to let her blow off steam uninterruptedly. He had never seen her so enraged, and he became subdued, quietly gauging the situation. He was mature enough to know that he would not win this argument and so *'e din pick 'e teet*. He agreed that they would move at the end of the month and that his dealings with Jennifer would be limited to telephone calls. When the child came, they could make other arrangements, he said. To this, Evadne emitted an eloquent "Hmmph!"

For the time being at least, they seemed to have reached an uneasy compromise, but he knew this would not be the end of it. When they got back to Cortelyou, Evadne was nauseous again. She went to the bathroom where she heaved the dinner that she had just consumed in the little Caribbean cookshop. Two weeks later, they discovered that little Hope was on the way.

CHAPTER SEVEN

At the end of the month following this discussion, she and Compton moved to the apartment on Ocean Avenue. As soon as they told her they were leaving, his aunt—Aunt Mildred—started a campaign of none too subtle harassment against Evadne. Where before, she was content to virtually ignore Evadne, she changed her approach. For no particular reason, in Evadne's presence, she would steupse her teeth in exasperation over some unknown irritation. She appeared to blame Evadne solely for their impending departure, which prospect she seemed to interpret as a personal snub. When she needed to communicate with Evadne, she would do so rudely. Sometimes she resorted to *t'rowin' remarks* in her general direction. To emphasize her displeasure, she would sing meaningful verses from hymns and popular songs, verses which told of the wicked, ungrateful, and guileful, all who would inevitably encounter some form of retribution.

Evadne had once overheard Aunt Mildred on the phone pointedly telling her listener about "*Dese* people Dese people dem who jus' come off de boat! Home? Deh en' got a pot to pee in; dem is po, po-ass people home, an' deh want to come hey an' tun up deh nose an' *play great.* Ay yai yai! *Yai! Yai!* Missis?"

Then she would laugh with exaggerated scorn.

In all this, his aunt's attitude to Compton never changed; to him, she was as sweet and considerate as she had been before Evadne's arrival. I imagine that as well as Compton's departure, his aunt deeply resented the loss of income that would ensue from it. After all, life in Brooklyn was no bed of roses for an unskilled Black woman in later middle-age.

To get to their new apartment, Evadne and Compton had to pick their way through the trash on the street outside, past paper that the chilly November wind blew into their faces, and along the loiterers who stood around the doorway and in the lobby area, smoking 'pot' or sometimes leaning on the iron railings outside with toothpicks dangling from the corners of their mouths. Occasionally, one of them would approach a passer-by with a "Romex" watch that he had for sale. Often unemployed, these men were from countries like Guyana, Barbados, Belize, Jamaica, Trinidad, Haiti, and Panama. They washed up in Brooklyn by all kinds of circuitous currents—one had been a waiter on a cruise ship that had docked in Miami; another had come up through Central America on a succession of vehicles and entered surreptitiously in San Diego; another who had been an insurance agent in Barbados had come to New York on a long expired visitor's visa—and so it went. They all shared a realization that it was growing more difficult for them to make it in their respective homelands and, initially, a hope that if they held on long enough in Brooklyn, something would happen to change their luck.

For them, Brooklyn was New York and New York was America. They had little personal interest in areas outside the state except to the extent that some close relatives or *pard-nuhs* would have wandered off the beaten track and established domicile in Washington, D.C. or Miami or Atlanta. In the Fall chill, their accents and dialects recalled down-home laughter, warm sunshine and sea breezes, but there was a deadness in the eyes of many, a desolation that bespoke a slow siphoning of hope. Some were known by nicknames related to their native countries. Among them, one would be sure to find a 'Trini' or a 'Ja-man', a 'G.T.' or a 'Bage.' In all weathers, in the morning, they would gather on particular empty lots, hoping to be selected when contractors came by in trucks to pick up day laborers. Then the chosen ones would clamber into the backs of the vehicles to be hauled off to work for a few dollars an hour, perhaps demolishing some building in the city, Westchester or Long Island—unprotected in a fine, deadly mist of asbestos. In the early descending autumn dusk, they would return on the trucks, their rough hands showing bruised and sometimes bleeding knuckles, hands made dry and ashy by the cold, grasping tightly the side railings where they stood in the back of a truck. Tired, they would drag themselves back to whatever little room or 'cotch' they shared or would hang around the front of the building, talking with authority about women, cricket, and politics (local and international) until it got dark and too cold to be outdoors.

As Evadne's pregnancy progressed, these men shifted from making leering remarks when she came in, to being solicitous—holding the door open, helping her with heavy packages, and offering an arm when the steps leading up into the building became dangerously icy. She soon forgave them for their initial "freshness" and in spite of its physical conditions, she grew to regard the new place as a refuge. It was certainly a step up from any other where she had lived before. As the months passed and as her pregnancy became more apparent, she considered that she would no longer be able to work for the Steins and, as well, in the garment district. As much as she had grown to like the Steins, she realized that in a few months, she would have to leave them. Bending and lifting after going up and down subway stairs and climbing on and off buses were proving physically difficult. At least in the garment district, she could sit at a sewing machine and work.

As news of the Iran hostage crisis formed a panicky backdrop to the sound of her exertions in the bathroom, she continued to be plagued by nausea. She wondered why her condition was called morning sickness when, in these first few months, she suffered from it all day. Adding to her unease and distress was her awareness of the situation involving Jennifer. She was plagued not only by nausea but by curiosity. Having made what he considered a clean breast of things, Compton was in no mood to divulge any more information about Jennifer. He was not the kind of man who had the stamina for nagging, and he made it clear to her that he would continue to handle the situation privately. He thereupon addressed his full attention to the football game he was trying to watch, indicating that the matter was no longer open for discussion.

Evadne had forgiven him for these simple reasons: She still loved him deeply and felt strongly that he too cared for her. She profoundly appreciated his bringing her into what she considered, for all its now apparent drawbacks, a materially better life than she had hitherto enjoyed. They had been married only a few months, and she felt strongly the need to give the marriage a chance to work. She still believed firmly what she had told him back in Buxton that night when they had first met—children deserved *both* parents. For heaven's sake! Who better than she was an authority on that score? She felt that she owed it to the life that now stirred within her to remain with him and to try to make a go of it. Before he met Evadne, he had known Jennifer for three years, and it was natural to assume that his kindly nature might have prevented him from ending the relationship with Jennifer in a nasty, heartless, abrupt way. Evadne felt that what he relayed to her as the brief continuation of the association with Jennifer *after* he had met her (Evadne) was attributable more to his reluctance to hurt Jennifer rather than to any natural inclination towards duplicity—at least, so she told herself.

Evadne made 'Gatha as comfortable as she could in the small bedroom she decided that 'Gatha would share with Hope. They agreed that 'Gatha would use the week-end to *ketch sheself.* Later, Compton came home and they all had a drink of *X-M*, Compton pouring a few drops on the floor for absent friends like Eustace whom he had known briefly when he had just joined the prison service and when Eustace was a young policeman.

After all that Evadne had told her about their current relationship, 'Gatha was curious to see how matters appeared between her and Compton. He had filled out in the six years since she had last seen him and had lost the casual awareness of his good looks that had made him so appealing when he and Evadne first met. He looked like a man for whom the exigencies of survival in the big city were now paramount. A serious, more mature individual had taken the place of the young man who had fortuitously put his hand on Evadne's outside the Park Hotel that warm December evening back in '73. 'Gatha did not doubt the sincerity of his welcome, but she could not help but notice that he seldom addressed any comments to Evadne—indeed, rarely looked in her direction. It was obvious that their relationship had changed since the days six years before when it seemed *dat breeze cun pass between dem.* Evadne, for her part, did her best to make things appear normal, bustling around getting his dinner, putting ice in glasses. Yet, in his presence, her cheerfulness seemed feigned and shallow. 'Gatha hoped that she was reading too much into the situation, that she was allowing her imagination to get the better of her. She decided to cast aside her doubts, attributing Compton's distance to tiredness.

'Gatha was eager to work as soon as possible, and Evadne said that she would take her to the Steins who now lived in an apartment on FDR Drive at Twenty-third Street near the East River. Mr. Stein suffered from Parkinsonism, and since his wife, also slowly being debilitated by age, could not look after him, they needed someone they could trust to care for them. Mrs. Stein had called Evadne asking for her help in finding such a person, and in this respect, 'Gatha's arrival proved most opportune. She was glad but nervous about this chance to work that she got so soon after her arrival.

She had written Leon a long letter telling him of her intention to remain in New York. It was the first time that she had ever made a serious decision without consulting him. In her heart she felt that they both knew the unspoken truth that she would not return, but the understanding of it was so disturbing to both that neither dared broach the subject. In the letter she had told him that as soon as she found work, she would send him money and that she would do all in her power to get them all into the States. As she wrote this, she realized the monumental task she was setting herself. How would she even begin to do this when she herself was now an "illegal alien"? She heard the term mentioned sometimes on televised news— "Largest haul of illegal aliens captured at border! News at eleven!" It all made her feel like someone strange, someone criminal, someone from outer space—not human. She had no idea of how to go about rectifying her immigration status and feared the thought of going before immigration officialdom. In time, she felt, she would confront the issue.

She had very little money left from the *small piece* that Eunice had given her in New York, and she knew that now more than ever, Leon and the children would be in need. Leon had never made any distinction in his treatment of her children and their children, and she knew that he would do what he could to make sure that none of the children were in need. However, she did not want to burden him with the care of the boys. It was imperative that she *fine somet'ing to do* as soon as possible. Evadne explained that the Steins would pay her "under the table" and enlightened her as to what that meant. She also told 'Gatha about the Steins' little idiosyncrasies and what her duties might entail.

That Saturday night, after dropping Hope off at Miss Ida, Evadne, Compton and 'Gatha set out for a Caribbean dance in Brooklyn. At first 'Gatha felt guilty about enjoying herself in her circumstances, but Evadne and Compton convinced her that the dance would be a good way for her to relax before settling into live-in work. The event was a rollicking affair given by the ex-prison officers who had issued invitations to the Caribbean community and announced the event on posters plastered in and around some subway stations in Brooklyn. 'Gatha was pleasantly surprised to see many of the old faces from Kitty and its environs, faces of those who had left the country, some just a few years before. There were so many greetings—"Eh! Eh! Well gyurl! It nice to see yuh mek it to de big ehpple! Eh! Eh! Nice to *see* you!" The music was loud as calypso and reggae rhythms claimed the dancers and drinks flowed freely. In the midst of the gyrating crowd, surrounded by the sounds, the accents, and the people, 'Gatha felt like she was back home again. The rum warmed her homesickness as she sat there eating black pudding and patting her foot to the rhythm, joining the choruses of calypsoes, and, in the mirror across the hall, admiring herself in the new dress Evadne had bought her on Rogers Avenue that morning. As the evening wore on, as the music seemed louder, and as they drank, people talked more loudly and let themselves go—"Feelin' hot! Hot! Hot!" For these hours at least, they could soak their troubles in rum, become intoxicated with the beat of the music, and forget about their problems with employment (or the lack thereof) or with immigration. This would be one all too short respite from the relentless lockstep of their lives through which trains roared and cold indifferent winds blew in this the largest, strangest Caribbean island in the world.

That Monday morning at about ten o'clock, 'Gatha and Evadne alighted from a bus near an apartment building at East Twenty-third and FDR in Manhattan. Before they entered the building, 'Gatha got her first look at the shimmering East River and the Manhattan skyline with its monumentally impressive skyscrapers close up behind her. With the waning sunshine reflected off it, the East River was like shimmering glass and reminded her of her last glimpse of the Demerara when they passed through the village of Good Success on the way to the airport. One heard the occasional blare of horns from the street and from the river. It all took her breath away. For a moment, she wished Leon and the children were here to share it with her. They took the elevator to the twenty-fifth floor. 'Gatha had never ridden that high before, and she stayed close to Evadne, trying not to make any sound that would give a clue to the other riders, standing confidently staring forward, that she was terrified by the long upward movement.

"*Je*sus Lord!" she shuddered inwardly. "Jesus *Fad*duh!" as the elevator creaked gently to a halt on the twenty-fifth floor. "What a country is dis!"

CHAPTER EIGHT

At their first meeting, 'Gatha liked Gilda. It was evident that the small, older woman was suffering from arthritis, which made her movements stiff and painful. She pronounced her "w" sounds like "v's" and spoke with a slight German accent blended with American idiom. She displayed a bright, ready smile and it was evident that she liked and trusted Evadne, a fact which immediately drew her to 'Gatha. She and her husband were German Jews who, as young people, managed to escape Hitler's ovens after being transported to England in an initial wave of young people, separated from their parents, youths who were allowed to go there in the early days of the Second World War. She and Ira met and married in England, later coming to the United States just after the war at the invitation of relatives in New York. They were proud of the fact that they had never spent a day apart in forty years. Gilda loved living near the East River, just *"downvind"* from the Statue of Liberty because the whole scene reminded her of the welcome and relief she experienced—"da fu*hee*dom"—she recalled they felt when they first came up the river and entered the United States.

Initially, she and her husband had worked with relatives in the garment area, but she gave that up to take care of her family when she started having children. Her husband left garment work to seek a living in the diamond district where he did fairly well. She retained her love for dressmaking and dress designing. Therefore when Evadne expressed her wish to get back into dressmaking, Gilda had promptly put her in touch with her relatives in the garment district. Evadne's early orphaning, her being game to fight for her survival against the odds, her willingness to work—all reminded Gilda Stein of herself as a young early-war Berlin woman, desperate to find a niche in the world beyond the reach of prejudice, scratching and clawing for survival in the midst of destructive forces. She resolved that she would do all that she could to help Evadne, and during her pregnancy, she and Ira continued to pay her when she could no longer work for them. After Hope's birth, Gilda prevailed on her nephew to make Evadne a supervisor in his Forty-Second Street garment concern where she worked.

The apartment was well kept, lavishly and elegantly furnished with impressive sweeping views of the East River, Queens and Brooklyn on the opposite bank and the Empire State and other skyscrapers behind them. It was a sight as 'Gatha had seen it only by postcard. Now throughout the week, she would live right next to these views. Mrs. Stein (she preferred to be called Mrs. Stein) carefully went through 'Gatha's list of duties. After she had taken her over the apartment, she took 'Gatha to Ira's bedroom where he sat in an armchair occasionally looking out on the river and reading the *New York Times*, the paper shaking in his hands. In spite of the debilitating nature of his illness, he appeared to be pleasant and fatherly.

'Gatha agreed to work for them for five and a half days a week. It could have been five, but she settled on the extra half day because she desperately needed the money and the Steins appeared to be fair and decent people who Evadne assured her were "not bad."

"Yuh will have to work hard," she assured 'Gatha, "but deh will treat yuh right."

'Gatha's day started at dawn and her duties included walking the dog, attending to the personal care and feeding of Mr. Stein, making breakfast, washing, ironing and a few light housekeeping duties. In good weather, she was also required to take Mr. Stein out in his wheel chair along the long promenade by the river. Often, she would sit on a bench next to him, and he would tell her about his life before he came to America when every day as a youth in England, he missed his parents and other relatives. Then, feeling lonely and alone in a strange country, hearing different strange accents, trying desperately to learn a new language and to make himself lovable in the eyes of his foster parents, he learned early the necessity for *appearing* affable. He told her of his desolation when at the end of the war he discovered that his parents and Gilda's father had perished in Auschwitz. They heard that her mother was still alive in Germany but that she had lost her mind. For years, after several reported sightings of her, they tried to find her but never did. Apart from their children and grandchildren, he and Gilda were all they had of their past.

'Gatha felt moved by their lives and wondered if she and Leon would ever be given the chance for what she considered such a rare gift of living. When Ira first came to America, he joined the Communist Party only to be subjected later to the McCarthyite persecution of suspected Communists in the early fifties. He said then the luster on the image of American-style freedom that he had so carefully polished as a German refugee in England during the war, was severely tarnished. He felt that he had escaped the hounds of Hitler only to run into the malice of McCarthyism. In the years following, however, he was able to recoup the losses he suffered when his employment was affected. Unlike his wife, he had mixed views about his initial encounter with "freedom."

'Gatha would show him pictures of Leon and her children and tell him about Leon's goodness, the twins' "own-way-ness" ("Deh own-way yuh know, *very* own way an' con-*tray-ry?*") and her boys' quiet resilience and dependability. As she grew to know him better, she told him about Eustace and the trauma she and her children carried from his violent death.

"You need to see them again soon," he advised. "Not only do they need you. *You* need them. Life does not give you much chance to make up for time lost away from your children. They pass through your life pretty fast, believe me."

He was telling *her*! Could it be that at night he heard when she tried to stifle her sobs trying desperately to keep the sound of their voices in her memory? Did he know that she stared for long periods at her boys' photographs and imagined what they would be doing and saying now? That she would develop a cold after hearing that the girls' asthma was acting up? They lived always inside her—right under her heart.

On a typical day with the Steins, 'Gatha was exhausted by ten o'clock in the evening and often fell gratefully into bed. After a while, to her, the East River and Manhattan Skyline lost their interest and novelty. Josefina, a middle-aged Puerto Rican woman, cleaned and cooked dinner. For all her years in the Bronx, her English remained severely and painfully limited. She resorted to teaching 'Gatha to communicate with her in Spanish (as she had the Steins) and 'Gatha tried to teach her English heavily laced with Guyanese Creole.

In the two years that she worked for the Steins, 'Gatha remained focused on those she left behind in Guyana. Every month, she and Leon wrote to each other; she faithfully sent money home, and near Compton and Evadne, rented a small studio apartment which she fixed up with a sofa bed, small second-hand chrome dining table with two battered chrome chairs, a second-hand recliner and small television set. At a flea market in Brooklyn, she secured cheap pictures of St. George's Cathedral and Stabroek Market, prints which she hung on the studio's freshly painted walls. Compton and Trini had dispatched a couple of cans of paint in little time. On a battered coffee table, 'Gatha displayed photographs of Leon and the children dressed in clothing that she had sent home in barrels through a Caribbean shipper in Brooklyn.

Precious and Princess were growing and losing their babyish looks. The boys looked like young men.

Living-in at the Steins, she was able to save a bit more than if she were working in some other capacity. Of course, the little studio paled in comparison with the Steins' apartment, but she was so proud of it that on Easter Sunday in 1980, the year following her arrival, she invited Compton and Evadne, another couple she met at Miss Ida's church, Miss Ida and me to lunch.

That Spring evening as the first tulips fought the frost in tiny Brooklyn gardens, we, all Kitticians (except for Compton), sat around squeezed together in the modest little studio, talking, laughing and exchanging memories and *tantalize* about the *mudflat*. I could not help thinking how much 'Gatha had changed since that winter night on the train when, soon after her arrival, I had met her again. She had lost weight and now dressed if not with elegance, with understated glamour. Her very manner seemed more studied, deliberate and toned down. I had the feeling that she was quietly observing her new surroundings and cutting her cloth accordingly. In spite of her limited prospects as an "illegal," she persisted in dreams of a continuing future in the United States, aspirations which she nursed and preserved for her family like Ovaltine she kept warm on a rusty oil stove. She never let go of the possibility that they could—would come to America, and all her efforts appeared to be fully focused on making that a reality. She used Creole less, making more attempts at Standard English, reading more.

After lunch, as the wailing of police sirens sounded periodically in the neighborhood, Miss Ida persuaded us to join hands while she said a prayer. The years had taken their toll, as we who had known her since we were small children realized. The older we got, the more it seemed that we appreciated her: She who had saved me from drowning when I was five; she who had been among those who cared for 'Gatha's children when their mother despaired; she who had watched the village's children like a protective hen.

Her eyes, tightly and earnestly closed, her words tumbled out vehemently on top of each other, increasing in volume as she prayed; her bony frame became greatly animated as her rather fussy, feathery hat trembled and shifted ever so slightly while she shook her head to punctuate her demands of the almighty. She had worn the hat to church that morning and saw no reason to remove it during lunch. She implored "Father God" to spread his protective arms over 'Gatha, to promote her endeavors; she prayed for those we left behind, that the struggle would not consume them; that we would surmount the hurdles encountered in the new country. She ended with a spirited exhortation that we should each be our brother's keeper and that we should not be swayed by the temptations in the treacherous world around us. That Spring afternoon, with so much love and long ago and *joie de vivre* in the room, how could we imagine that in the next year, for two of us in the room, life would have ended tragically?

PART TWO
*"Woman alone like kyalabash: Ev'rybaddy wan
pass an' dip deh han'."*

Guyanese Creole Saying

CHAPTER NINE

Columbia consumed my attention as I applied myself to the unrelenting rounds of exams and thoughts of where I would work once I completed the graduate program. My impressions of the campus remained ambivalent. I felt culturally disconnected from it, but loved Butler library, with its smell of paper and dust—Butler, which satisfied my hunger to know more. I loved also the stimulus of visiting lecturers who had made policy related to countries like Guyana, some who had never been able (or willing) to come to terms with discrepant cultural experiences alien to their understanding. People trapped in the disposition of always framing the world in terms of the Western metropole. Gradually, I stopped thinking of development from the dry-as-dust-paper-and-ink perspective of the academy and gradually saw it more in terms of flesh and blood people like 'Gatha and Evadne who were caught in its cracks, whose yearnings went unheard amid the clickety-clack complacency of the well heeled.

Being busy, I had no contact with either of them for many months. Then, having some free time in the summer, I called 'Gatha. She told me that, as her employers, the Steins had proposed sponsoring her in order to legitimize her immigration status. I thought that she would be ecstatic. Certainly this would make possible her reuniting with her family, something I gathered that she had been working diligently towards. However, underneath the satisfaction she expressed, I detected in her voice a note of reservation. When I said that she did not seem as encouraged as I assumed she would have been, she suggested that we meet somewhere. She had some other news, which she did not wish to disclose then because she did not want Josefina to overhear her conversation. "In dis place," she whispered. "Yuh kyan let everybody know yuh business."

I told her that I'd meet her at a Chock Full O' Nuts near Thirty-fourth Street on a Saturday noon just before she returned to Brooklyn, and she hung up abruptly. She arrived at the coffee shop looking very trendy in sunglasses, a straw hat, form-hugging jeans, short-sleeved sweater, and open-toed sandals. Again—I was struck by her slow physical transformation.

We ordered coffee and I asked, "So how's everything?"

She had met someone. He was twenty-nine to her nearly forty. Remembering Leon and her plan to "bring him up"—and surprised by her disclosure, I nearly choked on my coffee.

"Wh-what about Leon?" I stammered as I reached for a napkin.

She did not answer my question, but proceeded to talk about how her life had changed in the past few months. After the novelty of New York had worn off and the rigors and routine of work had set in, she realized how lonely she felt. The frequency of Leon's letters decreased—as did their length. After a while, his endearments became neutral wishes that she "stay good" and "keep well," accompanied by more details about the children than about himself or about their prospects as a couple. She had heard rumors from friends of theirs that he and Doreen were often seen together. Even though she questioned her own feelings about him, she was enraged at the thought of Doreen taking over her life with him, but what else could she expect? She asked aloud. When 'Gatha confronted him by letter about what she had heard, he replied six weeks later saying simply that she should not listen to idle, trifling rumor-mongers, but he gave no real assurances.

One Saturday morning, she said, while she stood in one of two long lines in a neighborhood supermarket where she had gone to get a few items for Josefina, she marveled in irritation at the check-out clerk's slowness, steupsing her teeth occasionally and patting her foot impatiently. She needed to get back to Twenty-third Street and hand the items to Josefina so that she could start her week-end early in Brooklyn.

Under his breath, a male voice behind her said, "Yeah. She sure *is* taking her time. She's probably about the slowest thing since Adam raped Eve."

Under normal circumstances, 'Gatha would have found this last utterance blasphemously inappropriate, and she turned slowly to see a rather good-looking African-American man of about twenty-nine standing in line behind her. She glanced at him and smiled faintly but kept silent and stopped patting her foot.

She assumed that he lived in the Steins' building because sometimes, she had seen him, emerging from an apartment on the twentieth floor, nattily dressed in business attire. On at least two occasions, she had held the elevator door for him, and he walked briskly down the corridor and entered it gratefully, mildly exuding a polished manner that she rarely encountered in the men of her acquaintance and a fragrance of what smelled like *Brut*. At other times, she rode the elevator with him, and they nodded politely to each other. While she walked the dog, she had often seen him jogging along the promenade. They had smiled as they approached each other. As was her attitude to the other occupants of the building, 'Gatha was polite but said little or nothing. She was acutely aware of her position as the hired help and had no wish to *step out of her crease* and be humiliated. She said that you could sense the reserve in some of the tenants when they came upon her in the elevator.

"I've seen you quite a few times in this supermarket and in our building," he said after a pause. "And since we appear to be trapped in the line from hell, why don't we talk while we wait?"

He was friendly in an open sort of way, which bespoke practiced self-assurance. 'Gatha forgot all that she had heard about being careful with strangers. As they left the supermarket, he offered to help her with some of her bags and suggested that she share the taxi in which he would travel back to the building. She agreed. The fifth one he hailed, stopped, and they got in. She learned that his name was Jack Feelings and that he was born in North Carolina where he went to undergraduate school at a small black college in Raleigh. Come to think of it, she said, he did sound a trifle different from New Yorkers she had encountered. He got a fellowship and attended graduate school at New York University where, specializing in Finance, he achieved a Master's in Business Administration. He worked with a large multi-national corporation near Battery Park and was single. (He was careful to work that into the conversation from the outset). He had gone on vacation to the Caribbean several times—with his last girlfriend. Their relationship ended when she decided to leave the United States to work for a company in Munich. He said that with each visit to the Caribbean, he loved the "islands" more.

"Well, yuh know, visitin' a place is not like livin' in it," she said conversationally.

"Yes. I know. Sometimes I think, though, that I would like to give up this rat race and head for a beach—sun-fun-rum."

"You can get dat in dis country," she said demurely, raising one shoulder and leaning her head sideways on it. "An' besize, you jus' startin' out. To me, you're a lil young to be t'inkin' of retirement."

She did not know why, but she felt the need to remind him, even indirectly, of the difference in their ages. She thought that his interest in her went beyond the neighborly and platonic, uncomfortably sensed it from their passing encounters in and around the building. Even though she was no stranger to the notice of men, she had never imagined herself being involved with a younger man—and one outside her culture and class.

"Like you implied before, looks aren't everything. Whatever you can get in this country in terms of relaxation, I am sure it's not like in your island."

"I doan come from an island," she said, taking mock exception. "I come from a country. Why people here always t'ink dat ev'rybody from de Caribbean come from an island an dat in de Caribbean, people jus' lie around on a beach, havin' fun, an' drinkin' rum in de sun all the time? It's not easy yuh know. People always feel dat de grass is greener in somebody else yard."

She felt a little hypocritical uttering this last sentence because wasn't this precisely why she was here in a yard not her own? A yard where she was considered undocumented, illegal, and alien?

"I'd like to know more about that *country* you come from Miss... Miss... "

She told him her name.

"Do you know that you've got a lovely accent?"

"*You* have one too," she said impishly. "In my country, *you* would be de one wid de accent."

"Which country are you from?" he asked.

"Guyana," she said and hastily added, "Not Ghana. Guyana. Guyana—in South—" She had been through this before.

"I know where it is," he said, before she could finish. "I travel for my company and as the token Black in my office, I'm often sent to the Caribbean—the islands *and* the countries. In fact, I've been to Guyana twice. Stayed at the Pegasus, in... Kingston, right? Near the er... what do you call it there? The... Benab, right? Two days each time."

'Gatha was pleasantly surprised to find that he not only knew where the country was but that he had actually visited it—if only briefly. The fact that he was physically attractive and personable was also not lost on her. Perhaps it was that she had not been near a man in this way in over a year; perhaps it was that she felt marooned and somewhat deserted; perhaps it was that he did not bat an eyelid when she told him that she was the hired help of someone who lived in the building; but by the time they got to Twenty-third, she felt more at ease with him. At the same time, however, her immigration status still made her wary of strangers, particularly Americans. Evadne, Compton and others had told her to be careful about giving information to those alien to her—not just about immigration, practically about anything.

"*Je*sus," she thought. "What a way to live!"

Somewhere in their conversation, she had threaded in the fact that she was a married mother of four whose husband and children were still in Guyana. Her life experiences had taught her the need for honesty early in situations like these. Momentarily, he looked slightly uncomfortable, but later she thought that she imagined it because he did not seem to miss a beat when he asked her to have lunch with him the following Saturday after she would have returned to work at Twenty-third. She replied that she would call him. (She was stalling because she needed time to think the whole thing through). He gave her his business card and wrote his home number on the back. Her thoughts were in turmoil. At one point, thinking of her family and reflecting that the moment she was out of sight, she would probably be out of his thoughts, she decided not to take him seriously. Perhaps he was just being nice and (her words) "really classy."

After all, she thought, she was nowhere near his league. To her, they had little in common: She was married, older than he, from a culturally different background and someone's uneducated, unskilled servant. He appeared to be a well-paid, well schooled professional who made a comfortable living, one before whom the world lay on a platter like a well seasoned oyster waiting to be topped off by a glass of white wine. He was one of the few Blacks (not building superintendents) who lived in this particular block of apartment buildings, and this boosted her curiosity while, in a strange way, leaving her a little in awe of him. For his part, I suspect that Jack (He turned out to be John Alexander Feelings III, but everyone called him 'Jack.') sensed something in her demeanor, in the way she held her shoulders, that bespoke pain.

'Gatha did not know it then, but she would learn more about him. Jack was no stranger to working class life. Throughout his childhood and adolescence, his mother worked, sometimes five or six days a week, as a domestic for whites in Raleigh, falling to diabetes at the age of fifty. Until his death from a massive stroke the day after he became sixty-one, his father struggled as a mechanic and part-time barber in Raleigh. While their children were young, both his parents had taken active part in the Civil Rights struggles in the South and had paid dearly for their involvement. In spite of financial hardship, they had loved each other and their three children unconditionally and were fiercely determined that they would be successful adults. The eldest, his sister, Esther Feelings, was a nationally known cardiologist in Greensboro and Eddie, the youngest, partially supported by his siblings, was enrolled at the United States Naval Academy at Annapolis. Jack and his sister felt that they owed it to their parents' memory to sustain Eddie during this period.

I felt that given all I knew of 'Gatha's situation and my earlier familiarity with her thought processes, it was highly likely that she *would* get involved with Jack Feelings. Don't get me wrong. I am not telling you that I thought she was naturally disposed to infidelity, and I would not like you to repeat incorrectly my impressions on this score. I think that she started out in the United States with the sincere belief that if she worked diligently, saved hard enough, and remained focused on her goal of being reunited with her family in

America, in time, her dream would be achieved and she would end up with a full calabash. However, the uncertainty of her aspirations; the difficulty and tedium of her days; the separation from her family by distance and time; the question of Leon's fidelity; and, most importantly, the ambivalence of her feelings about him coupled with her loneliness; all rendered her prone to the advances of a man like Jack who was able to look beyond what she did to who she was. While some would have considered it morally laudable had she brushed away Jack's advances like a *disgustin'* Demerara mosquito at sunset, I must tell you that ultimately, she did not. That decision would influence the subsequent course of her life.

CHAPTER TEN

'Gatha met Jack for lunch the following Saturday, and they saw each other for a few weeks before he invited her to dinner at his place. She felt diminished by the thought of her own shabby little Brooklyn *cotch* (the Jamaican who *limed* outside Evadne's building called it that), to which she had made it a point never to invite Jack. In spite of her getting to know him better, she felt uncomfortable during her first visit. She knew nothing about artwork; nevertheless, she found his collection, obtained from around the world "impressive" and his furnishings "elegant." She had heard those terms used by visitors to the Steins' apartment. After they had eaten a meal he had cooked, she moved to clear up and wash the dishes, and he protested sharply.

"Do *not* do that while you're in my place," he snapped. "You are not at the Steins'!"

She was stunned by the anger in his voice. It was the first time she had seen him lose his temper.

Then, pulling her gently to him, he said, "I can do my own housework, Baby. If I wanted a maid, I would have hired one."

Of all her children, Jack had been closest to Mattie Feelings. He worshipped her strength, resilience, and fierce love for her children in the face of unbelievable racist *eyepass* meted out to Blacks by Southern and other American Whites. Despite her tiredness after long hours of work, she still had time to demonstrate her love for her children, either through hugs, conversations with them, or an old-fashioned Southern whipping when she thought it necessary. While he was in graduate school in New York, she collapsed at her employer's home, working overtime to send him money. He always remembered her struggle, never shook off the guilt, never forgot her hands, calloused by housework and years of frequent immersion in dishwater.

His voice breaking, he impulsively blurted all this out to 'Gatha who gently put her finger on his lips and pulled his head down between her breasts. He reached up, for the first time finding her lips, his hands furtively then deftly moving over her body. That night in their nakedness, they discovered the delight of each other's secret places, the pure sanctity of sex without guilt as the differences that 'Gatha had seen as obstacles, seemed to melt in the searing heat of their passion. Punctuated by the distant, ubiquitous sounds of traffic on FDR and the blare of horns on the water, their ardor rose and flowed like the river way down below them.

Days later, she told him of the Steins' proposal to sponsor her and that once the papers were in order, she would need to go home to finalize matters for her green card.

"For years, many of these employers will keep foreign women on slave wages by danglin' sponsorship in front of them," he said. "Are you sure you can trust the Steins to keep their word?"

"I doan know if I can trus' dem, but fuh de moment, dey are all I have," she returned with tired finality.

"When I was in the Caribbean, I talked to people who said they got 'stuck' back there in the course of tryin' to get a green card. If you go back to get it, are you sure you'll be able to return?"

'Gatha was becoming irritated. His questions were giving voice to the unspoken doubts she had harbored all this time.

"What is all dis 'Are you sure-Are you sure'? " she asked with spirit. "Can *you* make it sure fuh me?"

He was quiet, chastened. He pulled her to him, unspeaking. Then she said with surprising eloquence: "*Now* yuh see how it is. Is like livin' in a strange worl' where *nutting* is certain. *Nutting!* Yuh have to trus' people you hardly know— de same way I trus' you."

Initially, they had no discussion of her matrimonial status and their future together in light of it. Then Jack began suggesting that she get a divorce as soon as possible. Mind you, I did not hear her say that he expressed any intention of marrying her after the divorce, but it was an inference that she clearly drew. Since I was not there during these exchanges, I have to give her the benefit of the doubt and assume that she concluded correctly on the score of marriage.

She never swerved from her original intention to sponsor Leon and the children if she got the green card. She felt that regardless of the state of affairs between her and Leon, she owed him that much. After he and the children came up, she said, she would discuss divorce with him for she was never fulfilled with him. Listening to her outline her plans, I had a feeling, which I did not voice, that to her, it was all very theoretical and that the prospective reality of a broken family remained illusive. At the time, privately, I also thought that while her decision to end her marriage might have been correct, it was hasty, poorly conceived and strongly driven by her passion for Jack.

Evadne, the only person in whom 'Gatha confided about Jack, made it clear that she thought the whole thing was a bad idea—"an' disrespec'ful to Leon to boot!"

"You shoulden turn up yuh nose, gyurl," 'Gatha protested. "At leas', you have Compton."

"Doan judge a book by de cover," Evadne replied, sardonically. "*Is mo in de mawta dan de pistle.*"

Evadne tried unsuccessfully to refrain from giving her friend advice. After all, who made *her* an expert on relationships? Like old milk, her own marriage was slowly turning sour.

"Dis is diff'rent from anyt'ing else I ever had," 'Gatha said with spirit. "All my life, I bin t'inkin' bout odda people. I cared for Eustace, Evadne, an' look what happen. Look what happen! Now I hear dat Leon *givin' me blow* wid Doreen. I am here workin' my behine off an' he home havin' a good time. Is time I start t'inkin' 'bout what *I* want."

"An' yuh t'ink dis new man will give it to yuh?" Evadne asked sarcastically. "At leas' you an' Leon have more in common. You all may have yuh problems, but yuh have yuh chirren together. Remember, *ole people seh, 'Teet an' tongue mus' bite.'* An' to besize, dis Jack is a lil boy to you, 'Gatha. A lil boy! He will jus' have 'e fun an' den move on. You t'ink dat somebody like he would stick arrung? 'E jus' usin' you, gyurl. I bet when 'e gyurlfrien' come back, t'ings gun change."

"Afta de lights turn off, all man an' woman is de same," 'Gatha asserted. "I have feelin's for dis man dat I never had for Leon an' dat I doan t'ink ever existed in me for Eustace. An' I *know* Jack care fuh me."

"Yuh have 'feelin's' because you t'ink Leon playin' arrung, an' a young, attractive man wid money showin' a intress in you. Use yuh head, gyurl. Use yuh head! Marriage is not a picnic. Doan geh distracted! Keep yuh eyes on de prize!. Mos' times as a woman, yuh have to *bear an' forbear.* Afta rall, when yuh decide dat you were not goin' back, I sure yuh din expec' dat Leon would stay by 'eself. Men not like women. Dey have deh needs. Look at Compton. I decide to *bear an' forbear* because all dis time, he *still* seein' Jennifer—an' I doan tink 'e *ever* di' stop!"

"What prize?" 'Gatha asked. "What prize? Married to a man I doan love, dat I t'ink now doan love me? Yuh mad, gyurl?" 'Gatha asked with a sniff. "I would *never* put up wid de shit I see Compton givin' you to eat."

"Yes, but you doin' de same t'ing," Evadne countered. *"Do suh na like suh."*

Because of their long friendship and her certainty that Evadne had her best interests at heart, 'Gatha did not take exception to Evadne's comments. She told me later that she tried to make Evadne understand how much she had missed a man's touch, his caring, the warm, deep, breathy passion of his voice—all that betokened sexuality, that made her human, that she could see ebbing away in the floodtide of an alien twilight. She told me simply that she clung to Jack because doing so helped her "to stay alive." How strange, I thought, that she felt so compelled to justify her actions to Evadne and me, we who had no control over her future.

'Gatha had done all she could to keep the affair with Jack secret from the Steins, but, unknown to her, Mr. Stein saw through her attempts to conceal it. After all, he was afflicted with Parkinson's, not blindness. Josefina, also, for all her apparent inability to communicate in English, was not without the means of transmitting her suspicions to Mrs. Stein. Of course, it was really none of their business, but they had all grown attached to this hard-working, determined woman. While the Steins quietly understood that loneliness might have driven 'Gatha into Jack's arms, they felt that it was urgent that they do what they could to reunite her with her husband and children. They contacted their lawyer who set in train the legalities necessary at the New York end of her bid for immigrant status. In a few months, 'Gatha would leave New York for Guyana where it was expected that she would "pick up her papers" at the United States Embassy in Georgetown.

In an effort to make Jack aware of all the dimensions of her life, she invited him, for the first time, to visit her Brooklyn apartment the night before she left. Sitting on the sofa and crossing his long, well-tailored legs, he made himself comfortable in the shabby little box of a place, which she had done her utmost to transform into a home. Home where she fought an unending battle with cockroaches, which kept migrating to her apartment from nearby dwellings, and with rats, which woke residents in the middle of the night when they rattled garbage cans in the nearby graffiti-scarred alley that reeked of urine. At the last moment, she had gotten cold feet and withdrawn the invitation, but Jack waved aside her excuse and insisted on visiting. In any event, she thought, after this, if he had second thoughts about their relationship, her forthcoming absence would give him time to think.

When he arrived, if he was putting on an act, he did a superb job. He did not appear in the slightest bit discomfited. As a gift before her departure, he handed her a pair of gold bangles in a gold satin-lined black velvet box, bangles that he had specially made and inscribed on the insides with her initials. He knew that Guyanese women liked to wear them, and he had noticed that she had none. As he placed them on her wrist, tears stung her eyes because no one had ever given her anything that expensive. He did not want her to go, but he realized that she had to. Now in New York, she was like a bird with clipped wings. He had to let her go so she might be able to fly back to him strong and secure. He clearly understood the tenuous nature of her immigration status and her constant, nagging worry about being away from her children. At this point, with her being already married, he could not offer her the immigrant protection of marriage to him. Besides, privately, I felt that he had not yet arrived at that place in his thinking about their relationship.

That night, also, some of her friends in Brooklyn brought little packages for her to take home for their relatives. Jack helped her to squeeze them into her luggage along with items that she had gotten for her family. Soon after she started working, she had begun to *throw a box* with Evadne, Compton, Miss Ida and Miss Ida's son. The *box* was a culturally traditional method of saving that Jack referred to as "primitive" until he considered that as an "undocumented alien," banks were inaccessible to her. His eyes were gradually being opened to her situation. The *box hand* she had just drawn, along with money that she had saved, would constitute her spending money.

There was additional money, amounting to two thousand dollars, that she had been able to put aside. This came in her off hours from baby-sitting and other services for persons in the Steins' apartment building. At first, as the sum grew, she hid it in a plastic container in her refrigerator figuring that that was the last place a thief would look—until one night on the ten o'clock news on Channel Five, she saw that others had thought of the idea. One day the back of her old television set dropped off, and she stashed the cash inside the set before replacing the back of it. Now she felt a little more at ease.

In addition to the material benefit she had seen in her remaining in New York, I suspect also that she seized upon not returning to Guyana as a chance for a sabbatical from her marriage, an opportunity for her to sort out her feelings for Leon. Being in America had wrought a slow change in her. She told me that even had she not met Jack, her time in New York had convinced her that she could not live the rest of her life with Leon, a man for whom she had no deep feelings. On the one hand, I thought that she might have been melodramatic and impractical. After all, all around us the world reverberated with the silent screams of those suffering from spousal remorse— but who appeared, nevertheless, to be surviving. On the other hand, I had never seen her so passionate and certain as she was in her belief in this glorious thing that she had discovered with Jack, this that she feared might elude her for the rest of her life.

On Tuesday, January 20, 1981, the last fifty-two American hostages were freed in Teheran. That same day, exactly as the fortieth American President was being sworn into office, a President who declared that "we must act today to preserve tomorrow," 'Gatha left a freezing JFK for the warm, sunny shores of Guyana. Of course, she did not know then the challenges that would ensue from this decision.

CHAPTER ELEVEN

In the nearly eight years of their marriage, Evadne and Compton were not happy together. On the surface, one might not have noticed it. Mind you, at various Guyanese social events in and around New York, occasions when you might have seen them, they made brave efforts to appear mutually convivial. But if you were around them often enough, if you listened to the *tone* of their voices rather than the content of their exchanges, you would barely discern the crack in the calabash. After Jennifer's appearance at Evadne's door that Fall morning in 1973, something irreplaceable died in their regard for each other. The episode was cruelly disillusioning for a naïve Evadne who discovered that there were chinks in her knight's armor. She had met Compton at a time when she felt most stingingly her father's rejection, and Compton's presence in her life was a salve to her wounded psyche. Jennifer's visit aroused the sleeping demons of Evadne's own insecurity, devils that she thought she had left back at Atkinson Airport amid the mist that shrouded the place. Try as she might, she could not erase from her mind the picture of Jennifer in Compton's arms, an image which haunted Evadne's love-making with Compton and was rendered starker when, on at least two such occasions, he accidentally murmured Jennifer's name. His refusal to give Evadne any more significant information about his relationship with Jennifer only served to make her increasingly bitter. She would *fatigue* him and *fatigue* him, but *'e woulden pick 'e teet.*

Confiding in 'Gatha, Compton would later claim that Evadne's cold withdrawal catapulted him back into Jennifer's arms. This was probably true. However, I suspect that Evadne's response also made it easier for him to act on what was already his secretly formed intent to continue the relationship with his former lover. Jennifer was moving into positions of growing influence with the company and was eager to help the father of her child. She spoke to the right people and Compton was awarded promotions, which led to supervisory positions in security. She was ambitious and, in the past four years, had completed a Bachelor's Degree in Business at City College. He admired Jennifer's ambition and her willingness to seize for their mutual advantage, opportunities that presented themselves.

With the passage of time, Compton became infected with Jennifer's drive and sometimes secretly compared Evadne unfavorably with her. He confided to 'Gatha that he thought Jennifer had "get-up-an'-go", the kind that he thought Evadne sorely lacked. In time, the very attributes—her being Guyanese, her reminding him of the culturally familiar—that initially drew him to Evadne were those that now gradually distanced him from her. Mind you, I am not saying that he stopped loving her. I think that in his own way he still did. However, when he compared her with the ambitious, hard driving Jennifer, he found Evadne to be narrow and provincial, not given to intellectual curiosity, easily intimidated by and suspicious of, the unfamiliar. To his irritation, Evadne sometimes sought existential justification in her occasional resort to "ole people seh" followed by a Creole adage. He thought her hide-bound in what was becoming to him moribund cultural tradition. She had gotten closer to Miss Ida and her church and, like Miss Ida, had an inclination to religiosity, which he suspected was more a crutch for personal courage and independent thinking than it was true faith. After the episode with Jennifer, he was relieved that Evadne "forgave" him and that she was willing to continue on in the marriage. Privately, however, he was contemptuous of her easy "willingness" to overlook his human limitations, a disposition which he came to interpret as weakness and fear of living without him in America.

For her part, Jennifer did what she could to pry Compton loose from Evadne. At times, she used her feminine charms, softly and cooingly trying to beguile him into complete accession to her wishes that he commit himself to her only. At other times, she became downright nasty, screaming her demand that he leave "the ignorant 'island woman' " and pleadingly throwing in a promise to help him further his education after they got married. (Such discussions always ended on the note of prospective marriage).

Compton was somewhat baffled by her demands for marriage since she knew that she did not completely fill *his* prescription for being "the good wife." On several occasions, Jennifer had made it perfectly clear that she was not, as she tersely put it, "June Cleaver." She was not, she said further, the kind of woman who relished the opportunity to gain her man's added love and approval by "slaving over a hot stove" every evening after a long, tiring day working outside the home. Moreover, she was definitely not the sort of woman he could awaken from a sound sleep late on a Friday or Saturday night to have her fix an "after-sport" snack for "de boys". Jennifer's main concerns were her child, Compton and her career. Being deeply interested in furthering herself professionally, she had no interest in having any more children and had undergone tubal ligation to ensure against that prospect.

Evadne had cornered the market in regard to what Jennifer was not. While emotionally, she had withdrawn from Compton, she remained unwaveringly committed to other aspects of her marriage vows. Even in the absence of a mother, she had inculcated in herself, seemingly by social osmosis, the survivalist behavior of the adult Guyanese women whom she had observed closely and from whom she had learned while growing up. Evadne might not have been a shining intellectual beacon, but she had an innate sense of what would keep Compton returning to her and Hope, and she acted on it in the best way she knew. Her home was a proud, peaceful, cosy, comfortable place deep in the throbbing Caribbean heart of Brooklyn. Her women friends, mostly raucous, prayerful, and vivacious, were drawn to it like candleflies to a flame. Concerned as they were with doing what they could to get through each day for themselves and their children, they did not permit themselves the distracting luxury of deep rumination about the decisions they made. They sustained themselves on hope and prayer. Like the fruits they preserved in liquor for the Christmas black cake, their lives, soaked in early and continuing hardship, had taught them about the nebulous and often elusive nature of happiness, and so they had settled instead for the prospective sweetness of survival. From a physical perspective, Evadne did what she thought would make Compton happy, even if at times it compromised her own comfort. She figured that at some undetermined point in the future she would consider the emotional consequences for herself—and Hope.

Compton might have continued to desire Jennifer but he felt that he needed a woman like Evadne. He liked his meals hot, fresh and home-cooked and had no patience with American "fast food."

"You doan know *what* dem people batterin' an fryin' in dat oil," I once heard him declare as he licked his fingers and thip-thipped remnants of food from his teeth while enjoying one of Evadne's delicious home-cooked meals. "Jus' de odda day somebody fine a roach in de fry rice at a Chiney cookshop on Flatbush."

He considered dangerous the activity of micro-waving and strongly felt that increasing incidences of cancer were directly attributable to this mode of reheating food. In addition to taking care of Hope and working in the garment district, Evadne was sure every day to prepare his breakfast and cook a hot, fresh evening meal. Weekend "night-outs" with "de boys" wound up at "his place," with Evadne uncomplainingly getting a good Creole meal going in the early morning hours. Compton had no intention of being stuck with two gyurl children. Yuh mad? When they could afford it, Evadne was willing to become pregnant again to try to "give him a boy." What more could a man want?

Yet, there was always Jennifer. Compton once told 'Gatha that even though he found Jennifer physically alluring and personable in other ways, he sometimes wondered uneasily about her motivations. After all, following years of a relationship with her, he had left her high and dry, gone off, and married someone else. True, they had a daughter together, but he could not understand why Jennifer appeared to be so fixated on him in spite of how it had all turned out between them. New York full uh men, he thought, guys who would have killed to be with her. Yet, she encouraged his interest, thinking of herself and their child, Joy, as his true family. He was as suspicious of her motives in continuing the relationship with him as he was contemptuous of Evadne for doing the same thing.

"De woman is a rail trip," he said, ruefully shaking his head from side to side with barely concealed pride in his own powers of attraction. "A rail trip. I jus' kyant understan' it."

Compton floated between Evadne and Jennifer, soaring over them high as an eagle, sometimes hovering in space between them, never landing long enough next to either to make her feel that she alone had won his attention. I would not say that he was indecisive nor did I get the impression from what he told 'Gatha or me that he ever gave the slightest thought to being committed exclusively to one or the other of them. It was not that he was unable to make up his mind; he simply had no intention of doing so.

One important bone of contention between Evadne and Compton was his attention to Joy, his daughter by Jennifer. After 'Gatha's departure, Evadne confided in me, saying that she had begun to extend to Joy her dislike of Jennifer. Evadne accused Compton of loving Joy more than their daughter Hope and resented the time, attention and money he expended on Joy. Evadne never said it openly, but I suspect that her own rage at the child baffled her. Nevertheless, her hatred gnawed at her gut—and, I believe, her conscience.

Imagine, therefore, her outrage when one day Compton declared his intention of bringing Joy into their home to *spen' out de day* so that she might meet her sister, Hope. Evadne was beside herself and flatly refused.

"You gi'e me enough grief arready," she hotly declared to Compton. "An' now you got de *idocity* to talk about bringin' dat woman chile hare? Yuh mad? I doan want Joy in my house. Soon it will be de mudduh! Eh! Eh! Well I tell yuh! Eh! Eh! Ole people seh—"

"She is *my* chile, too!" Compton yelled, checking Evadne's excursion down Creole Lane. "You of all people should understan'. Yuh fadduh nevah show *you* any atten-tion. Evadne, t'ink about how dat make you feel. T'ink about it, gyurl! Dat will *nevah* happen wid my daughter. She will know me an' know dat I love her. It will not happen wid *any* of my children. I love dem boat equally an' I will not for-sake eeduh one of dem."

Evadne was momentarily stunned by the passion of his outburst, then recovered herself.

"You kyan love Joy all you want widdout bringin' she in *my* house,"

Her attitude and utterances infuriated Compton, and he knew that if he pressed the issue, she would not be able to prevent him from having the child visit. However, years of living with Evadne made him question the potential cost of his insistence: He was well aware that she had finessed the art of passive-aggressive behavior, and he did not want Joy to be exposed to any disturbing situation. Besides, even though Jennifer acceded with reservations to the idea, she too was not thrilled about the prospect. He decided to let the matter rest—for the moment.

Compton's next increase in pay set him thinking of buying a house in Queens and "gettin' de hell" out of Brooklyn. He had had enough of the neighborhood where they spent the past eight years.

As they planned the move, Evadne was excited. It seemed that their lives together would be different after all. She looked forward to having her own little patch of lawn and, for the first time, her own house. Proudly, she was beginning to assess how far she had come from the little, ramshackle rooms in Alexander Street, Kitty. In her mind's eye, she had a vision of how she would decorate the house, the colors she would have for Hope's room—even the kitchen curtains. She became as emotionally attentive to Compton as she was at the start of their marriage, and it seemed that they were beginning to rekindle the old spark that had appeared to sputter.

Jennifer's sister, Faith, and her husband, Harry Addison, had decided to sell their house in Hollis. Harry Addison had become unemployed when the bank he worked for began to lay off employees. With the specter of foreclosure looming over them, strapped for cash, and requiring a quick sale, he and his wife set a rather attractive asking price. I cannot tell you with any certainty what assurances Compton gave Jennifer about their future together, guarantees that might have yielded the subsequent stunning turn of events. However, these developments would later cause Jennifer to relate what he told her, and I can only surmise that there was more than a kernel of truth in her account.

Jennifer said that Compton had convincingly declared to her his willingness to end his marriage and build a life with her and Joy. Accordingly, based on this information, she arranged a meeting between him and the Addisons' agent. Apparently, through the years, Jennifer had given her sister and brother-in-law the impression that Compton was married but separated from a shrewish nuisance of a wife who was making their divorce difficult. Compton himself had never explicitly encouraged these notions—nor had he ever actively discouraged them and set the record straight. Over time, his actions—and his silence—along with Jennifer's misrepresentations appeared to have left the Addisons fairly convinced that not only was he Joy's father but her mother's devoted companion of many years.

Envision, then, the Addisons' surprise when it became clear that Compton *and* his wife would be buying their house. Compton had thought that he would be able to close the transaction as the sole buyer, leaving his connection with Evadne unknown to the Addisons. However, the limitations of his own income and credit; Evadne's dogged insistence that she be included in the ownership of the property; the attractiveness of the deal; and his deep desire to improve his standard of living—all militated against his discretion.

For their part, the Addisons were strongly driven by perhaps the most compelling of all modern day human needs. Furthermore, their house had been on the market long enough for them to feel the financial squeeze of the protraction, and in the then prevailing climate of rising interest rates, prospective buyers were not beating a path to their door. Therefore, despite their barely concealed confusion, discomfort, and anger, the Addisons went through with the business. They and the Thornhills closed the deal in a strange, uncomfortable atmosphere. At this point, Evadne had no idea who the Addisons were, even though later she would recall that she sensed in them a discomfiture which baffled her.

Compton was convinced that ultimately he would be able to make things right with Jennifer. Oh sure, she would be furious for a few days—perhaps even a couple of weeks, but she would come around—she always did.

Evadne and Compton came up the Newkirk Avenue subway steps into the Brooklyn twilight. They had followed the closing with a celebratory dinner at the Caribbean Cook-Up on Nostrand. Now, as they walked hand in hand up Ocean, Evadne felt, for the first time in years, the closest thing to pure joy. To her, it appeared that in spite of all, everything would turn out right. There was a crisp, cold freshness in the air that heralded a not too distant spring, a sensation of life waiting to burst forth. Their walk down Ocean reminded her of the first days of their acquaintance in Guyana years before when *"breeze coulden pass between them"* and they had walked the streets of Georgetown at sunset.

Unlike then, though, there was about this Brooklyn twilight a strange otherworldly suspension, as if some great fate paused and held its breath in the instants before the descent of darkness. They passed a little storefront from which pulsed the lyrics and insistent drumming of the Rastafarian hymn, "Oh, Let the Power Fall on I." The far off wailing of an ambulance mingled with the sounds of traffic. Evadne shivered, but thought it must be the chill in the air. She was momentarily reminded of the assertive wisdom of Ja Man, a rasta who occasionally *limed* outside their building: "Chicken merry, hawk deh near."

As they approached their building in the near darkness, a woman emerged from around the corner and withdrew a revolver from her handbag. She held the weapon with confidence. In the style of the "law officers" one saw on television, she supported the weapon hand with the other, grasping the weapon hand from underneath to steady the revolver. She advanced in long, graceful, purposeful, high-heeled strides, stopped—and took direct aim at Evadne.

Chiney, a Trinidadian of Chinese and African mixture who *limed* outside their building, spotted the woman immediately. He said later that for at least an hour before, he had seen her passing periodically back and forth on the sidewalk. At first he thought she was a process-server for child support of which he was in criminal arrears, and he thought of withdrawing from the sidewalk.

Indeed, when they saw her the second time, his friend, a young Guyanese *boviander* man nicknamed, "Po-Great," advised him, "Banna, if I was you, I would mek misself scarce."

However, Chiney suspected that she had seen him before he saw her, and since she made no move in his direction he resumed his position with his comrades on the stoop.

As Chiney saw Jennifer take aim, he yelled to Evadne, "Duck, gyuhl! Duck! Duck!"

Petrified, Evadne turned to stare in the direction of the advancing woman. Even after all these years, she recognized Jennifer, older, a little more serious around the eyes, with a figure grown slightly fuller. In the passing glare of a car, Evadne saw her eyes, colder and crazier than they were back in '73. Jennifer's finger tightened on the trigger. Even in the cold, sweat popped on Evadne's brow, and all that seemed left to her were milliseconds of precious breath and all the sensations made dearer and starker when they are most likely to be lost.

As she aimed, Jennifer screamed to Evadne, "Die you fuckin' bitch! Die!"

Chiney's shout had made Compton aware of the situation. Compton lunged at Jennifer, taking her to the ground, deflecting her aim as the gun went off, the bullet hitting one of the graffiti-scarred walls and sending fragments of brick spurting in all directions. The group of hangers-on on the stoop had yanked Evadne away and formed a protective barrier between her and the two struggling combatants on the sidewalk. In spite of having been knocked to the sidewalk, Jennifer held her grip on the gun, and as she and Compton wrestled on the ground for it, the revolver went off a second time.

CHAPTER TWELVE

February 20, 1981

Dear 'Gatha,

Blessings in the Lord. Hoping the reaches of this letter finds you basking in the sunlight of God's love and care as it leaves me the same at this end. My dear, since you left many things happen. It hard for me to write them without crying. Girl, I wish you was here so we could talk like we use to long time and so you could tell me that it will come right just like I would tell you. My heart hurt so much, girl, if it wasnt for Hope, I know I would dead already. Miss Ida say that things like these is God's will and only he can ease this pain and I must trust in his everlasting love and goodness. Miss Ida say that she already call you in Guyana and that you know all the details. So I wouldnt write everyting.

Last week Monday night, Jennifer shoot Compton in his leg an' he die afterwards in Kings County. I never know that people can get shoot in they leg and dead till they explain it to me in the hospital. Apparently the police and ambulance they take they time when they hear that it was a black man who get shoot and in what area of the city. The doctors explain that the bullet went into a important artery in his leg and so he loss too much blood before he get to the hospital. I hear them saying something about toxic shock, but I myself was shock and I am still wonderin how me and Hope will live without Compton. Oh Jesus Lord Almighty. Look at my crosses. Just look at my crosses.

When you come, I will tell you about how the funeral go. The police have Jennifer in custody. They charge her with attempted murder and second degree murder. I pray to God that they will convict her, but I have to leave her at the foot of the cross. She like she thought Compton was buying the house for the two of them, but when she realize that he was not leaving me, she try to kill me and so everyting happen. The police promise to keep in touch with me because they say I'm a material witness.

We was suppose to move to this new house in Hollis by the end of this month. Trini, Ja, Chiney and the fellas tell me not to worry. They say they will get a truck and everyting and they will move us. God dont come but he does surely send. Miss Ida and Miss Sheila and some other people from the church they say they will come and help me pack. I know if you was here you would be a big help. Is so when you live good with people.

'Gatha Compton was not a saint but he and Hope is all I ever had in this world. He make bad mistakes, but we all make mistakes. He was only a man and in my own way I loved him. Even when I hate him the most, I still love him. In spite of what lead up to it, I still have to remember that by jumping in front of Jennifer and trying to wrastle the gun from her, he dead trying to save my life, and I am grateful. In the end, he prove in a big way that he did care about me and Hope. Maybe when I lose Compton, it was God punishment on me for washing my mouth on Jack. Girl, forgive me. I sorry bad. Hold on to Jack because he may turn out to be the best thing to happen to you.

Write and tell me how things going with your green card. Trusting in the Lord and wishing you God's grace.

Love from
Your friend,
Evadne

'Gatha sat reading the letter in the American embassy in Georgetown. She rose at four, and Leon delivered her in the *dayclean* dew to the long, patient line of visa-seekers outside the gates. As the sun rose and as the tropic heat slowly intensified, she stood with the others sweating outside the building near the Flamboyant trees that lined the picturesque avenue. By ten-thirty, she had gotten past the guard as the line snaked into the building, and she was later seated inside. The letter she held was tear-stained and a little crumpled, faintly bearing the fragrance of Evadne's *Jean Nate*. As 'Gatha read it, her tear fell on the letter, mingling with Evadne's.

An old man seated across from her saw that she was crying. He reached over, patted her arm and said consolingly, "Doan worry, gyurl. You gun get t'rough. Doan be fryken."

'Gatha wiped her eyes and smiled at him.

How t'ings could guh so bad fuh both uh we? She mused.

When she returned from the United States, she found that the relationship between her and Leon had changed none too subtly. At the airport, he greeted her cordially but like a long lost friend, embracing her warmly but kissing her on the cheek. She was confused, not knowing whether to be hurt and angry that he seemed awkward and somewhat distant or to be relieved since she herself was attracted to someone else. Oh, he tried to behave like they had not lost the nearly two years, that her absence had not irrevocably eroded what there had been between them. Yet he was always a plain man, not given to artifice, and she did not find convincing his attempts at affection.

Even more dismaying were the children's responses. At first, the twins did not seem to recall her clearly. Leon tried to jog their memory by identifying her with items of clothing that she had sent them.

"Remember de nice pink dress? Remember de black shoes? Remember de Farmer Brung?"

They were barely interested, but on the way home, she

put her arms around them and pulled them to her. They settled uncomfortably under the crook of her arm.

When they got home, tears stung 'Gatha's eyes when she heard Princess say to Precious who was trying to open one of her mother's bags, "Stop finglin' de lady t'ings! Leave de lady t'ings alone!"

To her own children, she had become, "De lady."

However, while a little standoffish at first, the boys soon easily resumed their interaction with her. They were now tall and straight with deep voices, just out of school and working as trainees with a government company in the city. One of them played the guitar at a local church and the other was a burgeoning national soccer star. 'Gatha felt a mixture of pride and regret that she had missed an important period of their growth. To his credit, Leon treated them as his own sons, and his loving spirit had filtered into them. They had just been employed by Guyana Timbers as apprentice electicians and, in their spare time, were always working at fixing some electrical device.

The year before 'Gatha's return, Walter Rodney, the Guyanese scholar-politician, was assassinated. The period immediately ensuing was one of intensifying political instability, economic stagnation and fear. In these difficult times, Guyanese working people proved courageous and adept at clawing their way to economic survival. Many schemed for ways to escape their own country. Apart from those like 'Gatha who 'jumped ship' once they got to America, some went to immediately neighboring Suriname, Cayenne, and even Brazil; others to Trinidad, Barbados, St. Lucia, and Antigua, places which decades before, some Guyanese had regarded scoffingly as "small islands," areas now grown attractive in the frantic stampede from what they saw as chaos. Out of this desperation, there emerged a growing band of "traders"—Guyanese who would travel to New York or the Caribbean to bring back for profitable sale in the country, basic items in short supply. A thriving black market in foreign currency flourished on Georgetown's sidewalks in the very shadow of the Government-run Bank of Guyana. Thus, many Guyanese who could not emigrate fought to make a living outside of the established ways.

While 'Gatha was in New York, Leon wrote to tell her that two weeks after her return to Guyana, Eunice had died. In spite of the onset of metastasis, Eunice might have lived longer—had she willed it. However, she decided that the battle for her life was not worth the effort. According to Leon, she was very matter-of-fact about it and never thought of her subsequent actions as a form of suicide or euthanasia—as far as she was concerned, her time had come. She had lived as best she could; she had no near relatives who would be crying buckets at the funeral; and she simply wanted to end the burden of living, doing so in the manner in which she always dispensed with problems—as expeditiously as possible. She had always held tight control over the course of her life, and she would too the manner of her death. The day after her return to Guyana, she summoned Llewellyn Gravesande, her barrister-at-law for twenty years. Having ended up on the opposite side of the courtroom from him and Eunice, her tenants and business associates were few who had not felt the sharp edge of his tongue.

Leon said that soon after her return, a weakened Eunice whispered hoarsely to Doreen, *"Mickase! Mickase* an' call Mr. Gravesande, gyurl! *Mickase!"*

As Doreen later told Leon, the telephone system was "in and out," and she could not find the "small boy" who would usually have been dispatched for errands like these. Therefore, she herself would have to go. She quickly applied deodorant, combed her hair, patted some *Mennen's* on her face, changed into a clean "frack," put on her good shoes, took her umbrella to ward against the afternoon *sunhot,* and went out to hail a drop car to take her to Mr. Gravesande's comparatively well appointed office on Croal Street near the Victoria

Law Courts. When she got there, she found that he had just returned from court and was removing his black robe. Short and a little on the stocky side, he smelled faintly of *Aramis*, his immaculately and expensively groomed person belying the general hardship of the period. After hearing Doreen's message, he promptly summoned his driver and ordered him to bring his car around to the front of the building where he got into the back seat behind the passenger side of the gleaming black *Mitsubishi Gallant*. He was about to leave Doreen (who was now standing forlornly in the *grass corner*) to find her own way back to Eunice's when he noticed that she was perspiring freely and looking exhausted. He paused and condescended to have her ride in front with his driver, Rupert, who was most appreciative of the generous view of her legs and cleavage afforded him by Doreen's position in the front passenger seat. Rupert rewarded her with a glinting, gold-toothed smile.

As a rule, with the obvious exception of his driver, Gravesande never let hired help ride with him. A Black, English-trained, Guyanese Anglophile, the lawyer was known to be of the firm view that employers did not elicit respect from servants with whom they consorted too closely. However, given the circumstances, he now made a rare exception. Picture, then, his surprise when Eunice later told him that she wanted her will to reflect her intent to leave the bulk of her estate to Doreen.

As Gravesande later told Eunice's physician, Dr. Veerasammy, when they met later for a Saturday afternoon cocktail at the Pegasus Poolside, his first thought was that Eunice's illness must have affected her judgment. Perhaps, he thought, the cancer had metastacized to her brain. She also had a high fever, and this too, he felt, must have affected her ability to think clearly. Veerasammy took a sip of gin and tonic and wryly assured him that Eunice was not losing her mind—not yet anyway.

By the time that Gravesande and Doreen arrived at Eunice's house, Eunice's laundress, Iris, was there. Iris was adept at carrying out her chores while positioning herself within earshot of the most confidential conversations conducted in the house. She was a Kittician who now lived in Wortmanville, and like 'Gatha, had been recommended to Eunice by Doreen years before. Iris afforded the village *spitpress* a special vitality by virtue of her being one of its most avid contributors. That hot afternoon, after Doreen escorted Gravesande in to Eunice, Iris situated her ironing board near the window (and the partly open door to the adjoining room) so that she could, as she announced, "get breeze." Later she would recount the entire conversation to her aunts, Edna and Ada in Kitty.

"Are you sure this is what you want to do?" Gravesande asked Eunice, barely resisting the urge to shake her.

"What *rass* you askin' me, man?" she replied hoarsely but, even in her weakened state, with spirit. "In all de years you know me, you ever see me unsure?"

Under ordinary circumstances, Gravesande never entertained anyone's talking to him with such brazenness—not even a client of some means. But he always had an affectionate regard for Eunice and admired her toughness, what he conceded once in an uncharacteristic lapse over drinks with his male friends as "incredible balls."

"But your will is so important that you may want to give it some more thought. You may indeed want to also consider giving something to the church."

Eunice pointedly ignored this last suggestion.

"I've given it more t'ought than you realize. You see how dis country goin'? So many uh dese people strugglin' to make it. So many people desperate. Which church helpin' dem? In all de years I live, I never see people *suck salt* like dis. *Hungry daag a nyam kyalabash,* Lou."

Here she paused, weighing her words. Gravesande knew better than to rush her.

"You see dat gyurl, 'Gatha, how she go to New York an' never come back wid me?"

"Yes," Gravesande replied, nodding with understanding gravity. "These people can be *so* unappreciative. Well, I tell you! After all you did for her and her family. You are a good woman Eunice. A *good* woman. But why do you again want to throw pearls before ungrateful swine?" he spluttered.

"I wasn' good enough. I make a lot of money, but I kept too much of it to myself when I was seein' want all arrung me. It wasn' dat 'Gatha was ungrateful. I knew when we lef' hare dat she wasn' comin' back. I wasn' surprised an' I didn' mine dat she didn' come back. I gave her de opportunity because I know she needed it an' dat she would have de good sense to tek it an' run wid it. She did what *I* woulda do in her place. She is not a fool. An' you know something Lou?"

She grasped his well-tailored lapel, pulling him closer to her lips because her voice was growing hoarser and failing.

"She knew dat I din' mine an' we didn' have to say a word about it to each other. It was an unspoken arrangement between us. You see, she was losin' her husban,' Leon, anyway—an' he had already lost her."

"Yes, but her not coming back meant that she was not only leaving her husband, but her children as well," Gravesande interposed.

Here Eunice paused as coughs wracked her body, giving her cover as she ignored the important last part of his question. A kiskadee fluttered in the mango tree outside her window. She caught her breath and continued.

"I could see in her eyes that her spirit was not with him. I could see dat dare was somet'ing in her dat would have died if she had continued hare. She was a good woman tied up in a bad situation. But dat doan make her a bad woman, Lou. Even before she lef' hare, I knew that her husband *eye was kyachin' fyah* for Doreen, an' I could foresee de problems dung de road if 'Gatha had stayed.. She din know about de two uh dem, but I did. Oh… Doreen and Leon t'ought they were hidin' it, but I live long enough to sense dese t'ings. When 'Gatha lef, it was den dat t'ings railly got goin' between de two uh dem."

"So do you intend to go to your grave rewarding adultery by leaving your belongings to a woman of-of-of such ill repute as she?"

"Hold on, Lou. As de folk song seh, 'Minna dead yet.' Remember de Bible that you go by says, 'Judge not that you be not judged.' "

Gravesande was losing patience with what he considered "this foolishness." His voice rose to a near squeak.

"W-w-why would you give this Doreen a *penny* of your money? She should not get *even a brass farthing*! Not a brass farthing! Indeed, you should have fired her the minute you realized that she was a trifling trollop."

Much exercised, he paused, wiping some droplets of perspiration that had formed on his brow.

"My God!" he murmured. "Still waters really do run deep: This Doreen looks like she can't even say 'prunes.' "

"Doreen has been wid me fuh years, and she has faithfully cared for me an' put up wid my foolishness. Furthermore, something tell me dat she and Leon will get much closer, and in a place like this, they will need to have something to live on. At leas' dis way my life would have meant somet'ing."

"I doan have time left to discoase more wid you, Lou," Eunice sighed with tired finality. "I t'ought de t'ing t'rough arready. I want you to promise me dat you will show Doreen how to hold on to what I'll leave her. It is time you start gettin' to know an' help po people instead uh washin' yuh mout' pun dem. One day dis country may get better, but before dat, somet'ing tell me dat it will get much, *much* worse. Guyana bleeds Lou. Guyana bleedin' to det, an' dare's a racist arrung every corner waitin' to get into power to continue killin' de country future."

She heaved a sigh that seemed to come from deep within and slowly turned over to face the wall. Her tone told him that any more protestations on his part would border on the obscene. Outside, a *jumbie* bird shrieked and a carrion crow swooped low over an awarra tree in the yard across the street. A northeast breeze blew through the bedroom's open windows, causing the plastic roses on the vanity to tremble. In spite of the heat, Gravesande felt a cold shiver pass over him, and despite his own disdain for superstition, he thought, "Someone just stepped on my grave." From the kitchen, to Gravesande's irritation, the unwitting Doreen who was peeling provisions for supper, started to sing softly,

> Bringin' in the sheaves,
> Bringin in the sheaves,
> We shall come rejoicin'
> Bringin' in the sheaves.

Reluctantly, Gravesande promised to do as Eunice requested and took notes while she dictated to him the terms of the will. He hurried back to his office on Croal Street and had his secretary type the document. Later that afternoon, he returned to Eunice's house in Kingston. His chauffeur, Rupert, and his secretary who accompanied him back in his car signed as witnesses. In the intervening time between his return to his office and his revisiting the house, Iris had apprised Doreen of all that she had heard. The latter *steupsed* her teeth, admonishing Iris not to "take people distress an' mek it *nancy story*." But her interest was peaked and she held her breath.

Following the departure of Gravesande and his employees, Eunice stopped eating, drinking, or speaking. In three days, she slipped into a coma from which she never recovered. On the fourth day, as the seasonal rains gathered force, pelting the Atlantic coast and sending derelicts and stray dogs running for cover, as thunder and lighting wracked the mud-flat amid a wild, noisy theatrical display, Eunice slipped softly back to the spirits of her foremothers.

CHAPTER THIRTEEN

Hearing of her arrival, 'Gatha's friends in the village came to visit. As soon as Leon's back was turned, they told her about Eunice Payne's maid, Doreen. According to Auntie Joycie, Miss Edna and Miss Ada, (Iris' great-aunts and Miss Ida's sisters), Leon now had a serious relationship with Doreen, the current owner of Eunice's house.

'Gatha had noted the changes in her own home. New frilly curtains hung on the windows; maidenhair ferns and hassar backs sat on mahogany plant stands; ornate crochet doilies lay on a new bedroom vanity, a spanking coffee table and new side tables; an Irish linen table cloth covered the dining room table; two new Morris chairs stood proudly in the sitting room; and in the newly rebuilt kitchen, an oil stove, fresh off the truck, replaced the old faithful Dover. Since Leon regarded many of these as feminine domestic accouterments that he would not normally have had an interest in, they indicated to 'Gatha, the spectral presence of another woman. Further, the broken front steps had been restored, and new louvre windows had replaced the old cracked ones.

'Gatha now wondered whether it was Doreen's or her contributions that had wrought these changes in her domestic surroundings. Aunt Joycie, always eager to enlighten, informed 'Gatha that in her absence, Doreen was a frequent visitor to her ('Gatha's) house and that Doreen "made herself scarce" after 'Gatha arrived.

After her return, 'Gatha hovered in the clutches of indecision.

On the one hand, she wanted to tell Leon about Jack so that she might be free to be with him. On the other, she questioned the viability of her future with Jack and wondered whether, Doreen not withstanding, she should devote her efforts to closing the gap in her own relationship with Leon. Now that she was thousands of miles away from New York, Jack and their affair were beginning to assume an air of unreality. Indeed, privately she began to question not only Jack's fidelity but also whether he had not merely been using her for a fling, as Evadne had suggested. She and Jack had agreed that in the interests of her achieving a smooth resolution with Leon, Jack would not contact her until her return to New York and she now sorely felt his absence. Oh sure, lying in his arms in his luxurious bedroom overlooking Manhattan, she had thought that it would all be so simple. But now, in looking into her children's eyes, she wandered the passageways of an indicting eternity that gave her pause, causing her to doubt her good sense as a woman and a mother.

As 'Gatha would later recount, at this time their efforts at lovemaking were self-conscious, contrived, awkward and half-hearted. Uncertainly, they rummaged through the trash heap of emotion, trying to pluck from it some replica of a relationship that, to begin with, perhaps they never really had. How peculiar this social contract called marriage. How strange the paradoxical strength and fragility of the emotion that would bind two people. She wondered how many, through the centuries on this coconut coast with mosquitoes singing occasionally in their ears— how many had lain awake on moonlit nights, doubting themselves for not being able to fit into the mould of others' construction, unable to tame their own humanity. How many women languished in a place not their own, yet smiled through unrelenting years of excruciating doubt? How many men had also done the same?

She and Leon both wanted to be measured in their approach to the problem of what had changed their marriage during their almost two-year sabbatical from it, and in so doing, they did not take into account the emotional difficulty of sexual contact in the midst of mutual dishonesty. It was like *tricky and tranney*. They tried to ignore the unsaid that lay between them, the *camoudi* coiled in the Morris chair in their sitting room— and finally could not. Leon brought up the subject. One evening, at his suggestion, they went to the seawall to talk privately, something that they had always done in earlier years. While they were sitting on the wall, he told 'Gatha all about him and Doreen. He said that even though 'Gatha did not notice it, Doreen always seemed to have an eye for him. After 'Gatha's departure, Doreen started coming around to help him with the girls, combing and braiding their hair, something he had tried unsuccessfully to master. Soon she was there almost every day, taking care of the house and, inevitably—him. They grew closer and soon, as he put it, he found that he "had feelin's fuh her." After she discovered that she was Eunice's major beneficiary, Doreen suggested to him that he ask 'Gatha for a divorce so that they could marry. Even though he had grown emotionally closer to Doreen, Leon was not yet prepared to end his marriage. He still felt some commitment (however altered) to his vows, and he harbored distaste for the prospect of being considered a man who would *hang his hat* in the house of a woman who would bring to the matrimonial table more money than he. That would never do in the eyes of his lodge brothers.

'Gatha did not know whether to feel relief or rage. She listened quietly and then she told him about Jack. She made it clear to Leon that her being with Jack would not get in the way of her sponsoring him and the children for permanent residence in the United States—once her papers had come through. Suddenly, he exploded and stood up. She had never seen him this angry. One of the qualities that had first attracted her to him was that, unlike Eustace, he was usually even-tempered. Now, he was perfectly livid and even in the

113

light of the full moon that hung over Demerara, she could see that he was trembling.

"Suh you mean to tell me dat all dis time you up in New York sleepin' wid a man? What kine uh woman yuh call yuhself? Whuh kine uh example you can be to yuh gyurls? I am hare workin' hard an' dis is what you doin'?"

"But Leon," she interposed, startled by his anger. *"You* were doin' de same t'ing."

"Yes, but I am a man!" he yelled. "I am a man! Nobody wun point deh fingers at me. Nobody wun call *me* a whore."

'Gatha could not contain herself.

"So den what would you call Doreen, de new love uh yuh life?" she asked with spirit. "She call herself my frien' an' look whuh *she* do. If you t'ink dat *you* are pure as de driven snow, tell me what you would call *her*? An' you—pointin' yuh dirty fingers in my face when as soon as my back turn, you tek up wid my so-call frien'," she sneered.

"If you din decide to stay in America, none uh dis woulda happen."

"Suh yuh lookin' now to blame *me* when all de time, you di' eyein' Doreen. I will jus' leave boat uh you at de foot uh de cross wheh I fine you!"

Then calming down, she said quietly, "Maybe, even if I had come back when I should of, I woulda loss dis marriage anyway. I t'ink you were sensin' dat when I lef' my heart was not railly in it."

"Marriage is a funny t'ing," he too said quietly. "Fuh it to wuk, it need to have *boat* people present in it."

After a pause, he said, " 'Gatha, I am not interested in goin' to America. I know dat every Tom, Dick an' Jack Rabbit tryin' to get on a flight out uh dis place. But somebody got to stay an' help buil' dis country or we will become a laughin' stock—a nation of people beggin' a lodgin', kyap in han', on odda people doorstep. You see how *even* de small islanders have de idocity fuh tek deh eye an' pass we? In de

Kyaribbean, ev'rybody hammerin' Guyanese. Allawe kyant jus run an desert dis po country. Wid all dese people leavin', is like Guyana lyin' in de street, hemorrhagin' slowly to det, while people jumpin' cross de body on de way to de airport. *Dis* is wheh I baun an grow an' is de *only* place dat I *evah* want to call home. Me an' my chirren will stay right hay an' rough it. T'ings will nevah be perfec' hay, but is home an' we will try an' mek de bes' uh it."

The passion of this patriotic utterance drove 'Gatha to sit up and take notice. Cynically, however, she wondered whether Leon's determination to stay was driven more by Doreen's ability to brace him financially than it was by patriotic fervor. 'Gatha did not demur against his choice to remain, but she felt uneasy about his inclusion of the children in this decision. She longed for her girls and wanted them to be with her. The thought of Doreen assuming a motherly role in their lives drove her to distraction. The boys were already grown and moving away, and she did not want to miss out on anymore of her girls' lives. Understandably, now she felt that there was no place for her here.

Even if Jack were not in the picture, there were other considerations. In Guyana, she had no skills that would earn her a decent living on her own—or no ways and means of acquiring them there. Also there was the consideration of Doreen's new position in their lives—the awkwardness, the embarrassment of it all in a small village. Further, in spite of the hardships she had encountered there, she had grown to love New York—the life, the hustle and bustle, the openness, the cultural heterogeneity of the place. And then there was Jack whom she could not get out of her thoughts. She was determined to go back and to have her children with her. She told herself that after Leon had gotten over his anger, she would broach that subject with him. As the soothing northeasterly breeze swept across them over the wall, little did she know that ahead for her, more problems loomed.

Sitting in the United States embassy, she heard her name called, and an employee guided her down a long corridor to a back office. As she followed him, her heart pounded and her hands trembled. She hid them by folding them in her lap when she got to the office and sat before a middle-aged white woman, who had been going through all the submissions enclosed in 'Gatha's file. The woman greeted her politely but unsmilingly and somewhat curtly, introduced herself as Miss Haggerty-Responsible-for-the-Issuance-of-Visas, (she said it like it was all her name) and wasted no time in getting straight to the point.

"I have some bad news for you," the woman snapped. 'Gatha's heart dived and she became light-headed. Her chest hurt and the pain coursed down her left arm. She thought that she would pass out, and sweat popped on her forehead. For a moment she was more overwhelmed by her physical reaction to the news than by the information itself. 'Gatha thought that they must have discovered that in New York, she had been getting paid "under the table." But it was something else.

"I have here a copy of your Police Clearance," Miss Haggerty said in tight, clipped tones, focusing her steely gray eyes on 'Gatha. "It records that you have one previous conviction for felonious assault."

'Gatha blinked. That incident involving her conviction had happened so long ago that she seldom thought of it. Soon after she and Leon were married, one of Eustace's women had accosted her in Bourda market. To 'Gatha, the woman's action seemed ridiculous because Eustace (and her relationship with him) had died some years before. However, it appeared that this crazy woman still harbored resentment and clearly belonged to the *"hyse up yuh frack an' buse"* school of contention. In the fracas that ensued, *she* first struck 'Gatha who retaliated by giving a fairly good account of herself.

In spite of the circumstances and because of the severity of the attacker's injuries, the authorities construed 'Gatha's response as "excessive." Thereupon, she was charged with felonious assault (a "big word" crime that she still did not understand). Being represented by none other than the eminent Llewellyn Gravesande, the "victim," charged with a misdemeanor (which was later dismissed), smugly regarded 'Gatha across the courtroom from beneath her bandages. Unable to afford a lawyer, 'Gatha stood alone in the dock. Her poverty and consequent lack of legal representation; her own inarticulate delivery; and her fear, ignorance and awe of the court system by which she felt savaged—all conspired against her. To avoid the possibility of heavy sentencing, she swiftly pled guilty and was fined heavily.

At the time of this incident, 'Gatha was much younger, and after it was all over, she tried to forget it and get on with living. Since she was not acculturated to the importance of official record-keeping and its surprising long-term capacity for stinging recoil, she merely thanked her stars that she would not have to spend time in the Georgetown jail at Lot 12 Camp Street or in the women's prison in New Amsterdam. In fact, she simply "blew off" the episode and the court proceedings that it entailed—until now.

As she faced Miss Haggerty-Responsible-for-the-Issuance-of-Visas, 'Gatha tried to stammer her way out of her situation. At first, she said that there must have been some terrible mistake. She vehemently lied to the gray eyes, saying that she had *never* been involved in such an incident. Then she said that she *might* have been but that it was the other woman who was charged and convicted. Then, after a pause and much spluttering, she said that it was coming back to her and that she herself had been charged in the case but had pleaded not guilty and that the matter was ultimately dismissed. Then she said…
The gray eyes glazed over, becoming steelier. Their owner sighed heavily, slowly and silently shaking her head from side to side as though she blamed some blind, insane destiny for posting her to this spot where there was no respite from sun or rain—or those who would mistakenly try to be slick.

CHAPTER FOURTEEN

'Gatha stepped from the embassy out into the brilliant sunshine and heat of Main and New Market, realizing that her hope for a green card had fizzled. Later, as she sobbed out to him the story of her rejection, Leon was consoling if somewhat distant. Even though resentfully, he saw only *her* as having been unfaithful, he knew how much her return to the United States meant to her and sincerely sympathized. He regretted that he had not had the foresight to try having the record unofficially "expunged" by one of his lodge brothers in the office that handled Police Clearance.

To his friends whom he met in a beer garden later that day, he kept saying, "If I de only *t'ink* of it. Bannas! If I de *only* t'ink of it."

Her efforts to survive in the United States and the hardship of her earlier life in Guyana had equipped 'Gatha with the ability to recover quickly from setbacks. Notwithstanding her glaring inattention to the significant detail of her conviction, she had acquired the ability to strategize adroitly. She began by carefully assessing the whole situation. First she decided that she urgently needed to contact Evadne. 'Gatha was determined to find some means of making her way back to Brooklyn, but in the meantime, she needed to safeguard herself against eviction from the little studio she rented there. She had paid one month's rent in advance and had already spent nearly two weeks of the current month in Georgetown. She next had to get in touch with Jack and the Steins as quickly as possible. She needed to apprise him of the situation and the Steins of her current circumstances so that they would, she hoped, hold her job for her. She would not tell them the reason for the embassy's refusal lest they think of her as some awful convicted felon (which in Guyana, at least, she was). At this time, the telephone service in Georgetown and its environs was not only erratic but also limited in some areas. Leon said that he had "put in" for a phone two years before and was still on a waiting list.

The day after the botched interview, 'Gatha went to Evadne's Nennen, Mrs. Gomes, who had a working telephone, and secured her permission to call Evadne whom 'Gatha had given a key to her place. Evadne was cheered by the call and eager to discuss Compton's death at some length, but 'Gatha had to cut her short since she did not want to run up Mrs. Gomes' bill. 'Gatha briefly informed her about the result of her embassy interview and the reason for her rejection, asked her to continue tending the plants in the studio, picking up stray mail, and checking to make sure that everything there was safeguarded. (She did not mention to Evadne the two thousand dollars that she had hidden in the television set). She then gave Evadne Jack's phone numbers and asked her to get a message to him requesting that he call her at Mrs. Gomes' the next evening at an appointed time. Evadne told her that she already had Jack's number because he had called when he saw the news of Compton's death on television. 'Gatha also asked her to let the Steins know what had happened and to ask them to give her another month to return to work.

'Gatha knew that at this time, some persons who "din get t'rough" with the American Embassy, would try to secure vacation visas from the Canadians. The next day, she went down to the Canadian embassy and obtained a visa application form. Since the crime of which she had been convicted occurred while she was married, she decided to apply to the Canadians as a single woman, and *walk with* her birth certificate as a supporting document of identity. She thereby obviated any mention of her incriminating married name. Confidentiality prevents me from revealing further the other means she employed in the submission of her application. Suffice it to say, that this new scheme appeared to have a reasonably good chance of success.

'Gatha planned first to set out for Toronto and from there, she would devise a strategy for getting into New York. Gwennie Braithwaite, her sewing partner in the sixties, had gone to Montreal in 1963 as one of thirty domestics in a program sponsored yearly at that time by the Canadian government. After living ten years in Montreal, Gwennie married a Canadian and moved to Toronto. Over the years, she had written often, inviting 'Gatha to visit her and her family in Toronto. From Mrs. Gomes', 'Gatha telephoned Gwennie asking her to send a letter of invitation which would be included with her application.

While the prospect for this mission's success seemed fair, there were problems. It took ten days for 'Gatha to make contact with Gwennie since she was away on vacation in New Brunswick. The Steins had agreed to hold 'Gatha's job for only a month. Josefina would assume the additional task of caring for Mr. Stein, but 'Gatha was sure that after a while, these new duties would prove onerous for even the hardy Puerto Rican. Her television funds would not last long after the next month. In addition, the Canadian embassy could not be hurried. Taking into consideration the number of persons seeking entry, one could not expect to get a reply from the Canadians in a snap. Further, after the third week of her stay, her funds were beginning to dry up and she felt a little uneasy. She had expected to be in the country for no more than about three or four weeks. Once, she glanced at the bangles Jack had given her and thought that if the situation became tighter, she would have to take them down to the Portuguese pawnbrokery on Robb Street. She quickly dismissed the thought.

In view of the circumstances, she did not want to ask Leon for money to hasten her departure from him. Yet when she considered it, she thought, why not? She was the mother of his children, and she was desperately seeking a way to support them. She had tried to talk to him about her sending for the children after her departure, and he adamantly refused to discuss—far less consider—it. He had taken to coming home from work, changing his clothes and going out and returning in the very late hours when she was asleep.

One afternoon, as she sat on the platform reading *The Daily Chronicle*, he wordlessly dropped an overseas airmail letter in her lap. He then got dressed and left. At first, she thought that it was from the Steins, but when she read the envelope, she noticed that the return name and address read: "Feelings, 15 Waterbridge Plaza, New York, New York" and recognized Jack's handwriting. Her heart felt like it had turned over in her chest and again pain darted through her arm. This time, however, unlike when it had occurred in the embassy, it was of pure joy. Tears stung her eyes, spilling over onto the envelope. He had not called at the appointed time and she had not heard from him in so many weeks that she had lost hope and was sure he had forgotten her. She started to sob uncontrollably.

From inside the house, Precious who was playing jacks with Princess, said uneasily to her sister, "Somet'ing happen. Mommy on de *flatform* cryin'. "

"Nutting en happen, darlin'," 'Gatha returned. "Mommy jus' happy."

She opened the envelope, holding the letter to her lips, relishing the faint fragrance of his cologne that still clung to it, bringing him closer. She wondered what he was doing right then.

She could just see him washing his own dishes, doing his own laundry, cooking and cleaning his apartment—then saying to her, "See? Doing these things is not women's work only."

Her hands shaking, she tore open the envelope and read the letter. A check also fell from the envelope into her lap.

March 1981

My dearest,

I know we agreed that I wouldn't try to contact you, but I couldn't bear missing you and yearning for your touch in the middle of the night. Forgive my "eye-docity," as I know you would have put it. (Smile). I also can't live with the thought of the disappointment you faced in the embassy. I think you would have referred to that as "eye-pass." Remember, it hurts me too. I love and miss you so much that I feel like coming down there and taking you away. But of course we both know there is much more to it than that. Evadne told me you're seeking other means. (I will not say more in a letter). I think she was trying to protect you and did not want to give too much information.

I realize how much you hate the idea of a knight in shining armor, how much you've "paddled your own canoe" as you put it. I know that every time you were down you've tried to struggle to your feet and be a brave woman warrior. But promise me, Baby, that now you will accept my help, which I believe you now sorely need. I regret that so much of your life has passed without me being there to ease the pain you've already been through. I am sorry about all the years we missed together. Now just when we found each other, it looks like we may be apart indefinitely.

I have enclosed a certified check for five hundred dollars that I hope will tide you over as you seek other means to return to New York. Sweetie, just say as you've taught me, that "God don't come but he does send" and use the money. You notice how many of these Guyanese sayings I'm picking up? Soon I

may be able to go into the Guyanese embassy in Washington
and qualify for a passport, no questions asked! (Smile, gyurl!)
In sending the check, I ignored Evadne's warning that I ran the
risk of having it stolen in the mail. She advised me to enclose
it in carbon paper before I put it in the envelope—or some such
crazy thing. I hope it is now safely in your hands. At least now,
you will have enough money to call me if you need me.

I saw the news of Evadne's husband's murder on the Channel
Five News at ten o'clock. I realized that she was the friend
you told me so much about, so I called her right away and of-
fered to help in anyway I could.

Last night as I watched the moon rising over the East River
in Battery Park, I thought how strange life is. There was a
time when they stole Black people from Africa and brought
them here under that same moon to work them to death for
free to build this country. Now, when other Black people
want to come to work for wages, they turn them away from
their embassies. My dearest one, don't let them make you feel
that you're any less of a person than they. You're one in a
long line of proud people from other countries (some who did
not come of their own free will), some who, in their own small
way (and in spite of their past) would struggle to make this
country a better place. You've taught me more than any uni-
versity about courage, determination, and most of all—joy—
something our people lost in the first crossing from Africa.
Something which in spite of all our music and dancing, we
are still desperately seeking. Something which you in all the
difficulties you've faced have not stopped striving for. Hold
your head up and do what you can for us to be together
again. Remember that I am prepared to do all I can on this
end if you need anything. Once you manage to get back here,
I promise that I will make things right for us.

Have you spoken yet to Leon? If so what was his response? What about Precious and Princess and the boys? I hope to meet them some day. It is now one in the morning and tomorrow I have a long day of meetings and reports. Call me. I love you more than ever.

Your own Jack

CHAPTER FIFTEEN

In the period immediately following Compton's murder, Evadne was in obvious turmoil. She showed signs of post-traumatic stress: shaking and crying uncontrollably, finding it hard to focus on matters at hand, to eat, or to sleep. Immediately following the incident, she was hospitalized overnight at King's County because the Emergency Medical Technicians who had responded to the call found it difficult to allay her hysteria at the scene. Detectives who arrived to investigate the matter could elicit no information from her so they had to settle for the eyewitness accounts of the stoop-sitters, many who were innately resentful of the police. Eventually though, Evadne's rage against Jennifer drove her to try to pull herself together to a point at which early the next morning, she was able to answer most questions the police put to her. At King's County, a doctor gave Evadne a sedative to ease the trauma and to help her deal with the coming days. She was grateful that until her arraignment, Jennifer would remain in police custody at the Brooklyn Women's House of Detention.

The links Evadne had forged in the church and the support she acquired from Miss Ida helped her get through the horror of it all. Running errands and just uttering encouragement, the stoop-fixtures fell over themselves to be of assistance. That morning after Miss Ida called to tell me what happened, I got on the subway and went over from Manhattan, forgetting all about the exam I was studying for. I found the apartment full of people who came and went (but mostly stayed), murmuring glib, obligatory statements about God and His disposition to be relied on in times like these. A local television reporter sat in a corner taking it all in while he munched appreciatively on a warm pattie from a tray that Gladys, Evadne's hairdresser and fellow church member, had passed around. Even Compton's Aunt Mildred had come, Aunt Mildred at whose apartment he and Evadne dwelled so uncomfortably during the early days of their marriage. She made herself useful, tending Hope, cooking soup, and insisting that Evadne eat and rest.

"Gyurl, even if is jus' a mout'ful uh soup, yuh need to keep yuh strengt' up. Try it. It tases nice," coaxed Miss Ida who now appeared to be the *chief cook and bottle-washer*. "It tases *too* nice. An' afta rall, yuh still 'ave 'Ope to live for."

Evadne sat in an arm chair in the living room receiving well-wishers, curiosity-seekers, and alleged hypocrites who, she told me later, had made snide remarks behind their backs that she an' Compton *smellin' dehself* to t'ink dat dey would *buy house* in Queens. Dat dey was *hurry come up an' po great, to besize*. Evadne's eyes were swollen almost shut, and her head was tied with a cotton scarf that came low over her forehead. Miss Ida had *nineted* and *sapped* her with bay rum and shilling oil because Ida thought that she felt feverish. The cotton dress that Evadne wore hung loose about her.

"Yes gyurl, drink de lil soup. Nevah mine. Nevah mine. *Neh-*vah *mine!*" Aunt Mildred *skreeled out* tearfully but melodramatically. "God's justice will prevail against dat *bitch*. Suh help me! From de firs' I see she when 'e bring she home, I seh to myself, 'Mildred?' I seh, '*Mildred*? Dis bitch is trouble! Dis bitch doan like cook! She doan like look afta house! She only like dress an' party!' [Mildred counted off each of these perceived failings on her fingers.] Wha' kine uh woman is *dat* to t'ink bout mekkin she yuh wife? I tell him, 'Compton?' I seh, 'Compton? Get a good gyurl. Get a decent gyurl from home, an' suh 'e guh an' bring back Evadne.

An' now dat *bitch*—she kill mi nephew. Oh God! Oh Fadduh God!" Aunt Mildred collapsed in a sobbing heap in a corner of a sofa.

Since Aunt Mildred appeared to be on the verge of hysteria, her middle-aged couch-dweller, Miss Desiree, always overly solicitous of her benefactress, moved over to fan her with a soiled, folded copy of the *New York Post.* Miss Desiree then called for someone to bring a glass of "sweet sugar water" since Aunt Mildred appeared to be on the edge of "fainting away."

I found Mildred fascinating. In a brief utterance, she had adroitly passed over a range of emotion from concern for Evadne, through rage at Jennifer, to personal grief. All eyes now on her, she turned theatrically to Evadne.

"Gyurl, yuh 'ave been a good wife to 'im an' a good mudduh to 'is chile. Yuh know dat 'is family always cherish you from de time dat you live wid us when you firs' come up. An' now dat 'e gone, we will stay close to you an' Hope because allawe is one family. Doan let a day go by dat you doan call on us when you need anyt'ing. *Anyt'ing,* I tell yuh! You know dat from de firs', we always live good-good, an' as deh seh, *'Han' wash han' mek han come clean.'* Oh Fadduh God!"

Evadne emerged from her grief long enough to shoot Mildred a cold, cynical stare. I sensed that much of Aunt Mildred's histrionics were geared towards garnishing as much attention as she could. The television reporter quickly brushed away pattie crumbs from his lips and furtively began taking notes. He then rose and swiftly tip-toed from the room out to the station van to retrieve his cameraperson.

The coroner's report pending, the police retained the body. Finally, with the aid of family and friends, Evadne arranged the funeral, which was held at the Blessed Assurance Funeral Home on Church Avenue between Bedford and Flatbush.

The viewing took place on a frigid, snowy, blustery evening in late February. I thought, how different this cold, forbidding, alien night of their farewell, how unlike that on which Compton and Evadne first met so many years before on that warm, tropical Christmas evening in familiar Georgetown. Despite the single-digit temperatures, the funeral home was packed. Mourners looked somber and talked in hushed tones, obviously discussing the event that led them to that place. Compton's popularity, along with the publicity and notoriety of the circumstances surrounding his death, drew a standing room only crowd that spilled over into the dimly lit, carpeted vestibule.

In death, he lay impeccably dressed in a well-cut, dark blue, pinstripe suit with silk shirt and tie, all of which he had bought three weeks before from Macy's in Brooklyn in anticipation of a wedding to which he and Evadne were invited. He had told one of his "ex-police" pals that Jennifer was with him and helped him select it. Her unerring sense of style was clearly evident.

Compton's hands were stiffly folded, and to me, his face looked strangely alien. Remembering how distracted he sometimes seemed in life, I was struck by the peaceful contrast now reflected on his countenance. It appeared that for him, all troubling issues were finally resolved and that death had at last afforded him release from an uncomfortably tight space and given him peace for which he had paid the ultimate price. Everything we had all thought of as important up to this point now seemed starkly irrelevant.

In the front pew, Evadne sat next to Hope, receiving the condolences of those who came up to view the body. Compton's friends and acquaintances, many who formerly worked in the Guyanese uniformed services such as the Military, Prison and Police were strongly represented. Someone had gotten hold of an old, crackling recording of "My Native Land" sung by the British Guiana Police Male Voice Choir."

Snow and cold holding sway in an alien land outside, the voices of these Guyanese men, many now gone, were heard in the background, softly, dolefully voicing the words of the patriotic Guyanese song:

> *And when at length I come to die,*
> *I want no gilded tomb.*
> *Just let me rest within thy breast*
> *Where thy sweet flowers bloom.*

For Compton, however, in death there would be no sound of soothing tropical breezes rustling through the *Le Repentir's* giant, sentinel palms. His body would be interred in the Cypress Hills Cemetery beside the unending traffic of the noisy Interboro Parkway, the place where he would attend eternity with other immigrants like himself, all now gone to their ancestors.

Evadne felt the touch of a hand on her arm. She looked up into the unfamiliar face of a tall, rather attractive Black man in an expensive-looking wool coat. At first she thought that he must be one of Compton's supervisors, come to pay his last respects.

"Hello Mrs. Thornhill. Someone back here [inclining his head] told me who you were. I called you earlier," he whispered. "I'm Jack Feelings, Agatha's friend. I came because Agatha would have wanted me to be here. She said that you all are like her family, and she's spoken so much of all of you, I felt that I knew you even though we'd never met. I'm sorry about how things turned out. I never met him, but in spite of everything and from all I heard, Compton was a great guy."

Evadne grasped his hand and started to sob. Jack's presence and the mention of her name reminded Evadne of how much at this time she also sorely missed 'Gatha.

"Don't worry, Evadne," he said gently. "If you need anything, give me a call. Here's my card."

He stepped away to give others a chance to get up front.

Then, Evadne saw Jennifer's sister, Faith Addison, from whom she and Compton had bought the house. Because it was so central to the events that unfolded, Evadne wondered if she and Hope could ever find happiness there, especially without Compton. Evadne felt a surge of rage that Faith Addison would dare to intrude on her grief in light of her sister's horrifying action. Then Evadne glanced down and saw the little girl Faith held by the hand and whom she led up front to the casket. Joy's stunning resemblance to Evadne's own daughter, Hope (just a few months younger), momentarily took Evadne's breath away. Being just barely tall enough to see into the casket, Joy stood for a few moments with her aunt, her little hands gripping its satin-lined edge, peering unblinkingly at her father's dead body. Then Faith and Joy both turned and came over to Evadne, and wordlessly, Faith put her arms around Evadne who stiffened at first, then relaxed. Unspeaking, they held each other long. Faith whispered something to Evadne and then to Joy who took Evadne's hand and then Hope's. After this, Faith and Joy moved on down the aisle. Few in the packed assembly knew who they were.

I sat a couple of pews behind Evadne. As Faith and Joy passed me, little Joy's eyes met mine, and it struck me poignantly that she had lost *both* parents. As one often sees in the eyes of the innocents, I caught sight of the mysterious, ethereal recesses of the past and the future. In them, strangely, I also glimpsed a divinity of which many churchmen speak glibly, but which few of them really know.

Later, Evadne told me she decided that after she had time to work through her grief, she would invite Joy (who was now in the Addisons' custody) to their home so that she and Hope would get to know her. Evadne made it clear that she was doing so not so much for Compton—but for herself, and she knew it would not be easy. She did not say this, but I think she grasped that her unconditional acceptance of Joy might ease the protracted pain she felt over her own father's rejection and might fill her *kyalabash*, taking her into a realm of psychic wholeness. After a long silence between us, she recalled musingly that the night before he died, Compton had reminded her that *"Pickney who a cry a house an' a door a same t'ing."*

For weeks after receiving 'Gatha's distress call, Evadne would take the train from Queens into Brooklyn to check on the studio. However, doing this regularly was not possible. Evadne was concerned with financial and legal matters related to Compton's death; getting Hope into a new school; her own return to work; unpacking after the move from Brooklyn; and adjusting to her new reality. One positive aspect of the whole situation was that once she was financially disciplined enough, mortgage insurance and life insurance which Compton had taken out would leave her able to manage fairly well. She was grateful that Jack had offered to help her in this regard and that he had also gone to Brooklyn to check on 'Gatha's belongings when she could not. However, his work required that he go to Washington for two weeks. One afternoon, she was startled to discover that 'Gatha's studio had been burgled.

When the police questioned the neighbors, they said they had seen and heard nothing. Indeed, they said, they were surprised to learn that anyone even lived there. 'Gatha's personal belongings were strewn throughout the rooms. The thieves even had time to cook themselves a meal. The police perfunctorily went about their investigation. They said these incidents occurred routinely and advised Evadne that immediately upon her return, 'Gatha should visit the Police Precinct. It was not as bad as it looked, they consoled. After all, the thieves had taken replaceable items like her toaster, her stereo and her television set.

CHAPTER SIXTEEN

'Gatha finally received the Canadian visitor's visa on April Fool's Day 1981. Jack's gift of money turned out to be a boon in her situation. The cost of remaining in Kitty beyond the time that she had envisioned was more than she budgeted for. After Evadne told her about the break-in, her spirits dived—but not for long. She contemplated her position—the possible loss of her family; theft of her belongings in the apartment, along with the two thousand dollars she had hidden in the television set; her possible eviction from the apartment if she were not back in another month; Compton's death; and her inability to secure a green card for the United States. However, she did not stay down long. She held fast to the hope and determination that she would make it back. Another letter from Jack, this one in care of Mrs. Gomes, kept her spirits and expectations afloat, and she geared herself to making an effort to regain a foothold in New York. This, though, was not something Jack could help her with. It was all left to her.

She contemplated that years before this, when Eustace left her with a full belly and an empty promise of marriage, she had spiraled into an emotional tailspin that threatened her sanity and even her life. Since then, she had suffered many more challenges to her ability to survive, but she had grown stronger and had not caved in.

Of course, by entering the United States illegally, she would be breaking the law. Yet, I don't think that she ever quite regarded her mission in that light. I believe that being now no stranger to difficulty, she saw it as a series of river rapids that she would be required to negotiate as she paddled her canoe upstream. Her experience in the embassy, I think, had bitterly sealed her distrust for officialdom (domestic and foreign) and destroyed any lingering misconceptions she had about the efficacy of strict adherence to rules—especially on the part of the socially disadvantaged. The words of the vendor kept coming back to her, he who sold lottery tickets on the city sidewalk outside Fogarty's: "If you haven' got a ticket, you haven' got a chance." Well, she had just used almost the last of her money to buy a plane ticket to Toronto.

It was clear to her that Leon was seeing someone else, and she was reasonably sure that it was Doreen. As if by some tacit agreement, they now slept in separate areas—she, with the girls and he, in the bedroom by himself. Oh, he was careful not to rub her nose in whatever he was engaged in, but she sensed that he had little interest in being with her again. Even as she thought she should not have minded, her pride was hurt. If he married Doreen, 'Gatha felt that at least the children would be taken care of. Doreen had always loved them as if they were her own. Yet maternal jealousy nagged at 'Gatha, the thought of another woman being so close to her children, filling her with dread and sadness. Neither Doreen nor 'Gatha had made an effort to see each other. It was like they had some unspoken agreement to keep their distance from each other. 'Gatha said nothing more to Leon about the girls' going with her. First, she wanted to get back to New York and see what she could do to straighten out her affairs.

On this occasion, she asked Leon not to bring the children to the airport. She felt that its crowded, unfamiliar atmosphere would upset them, so she said goodbye to them at home, promising to write as soon as she got to Toronto. As the car pulled away from the cottage, she watched them standing on the platform, the girls, their little hands gripping the rails as they gazed at the car disappearing around the corner. She and Leon said little to each other on the way to the airport. They both knew that if she managed to enter New York, it would be a long time before they would see each other again.

Among the passengers headed out of Timehri for Toronto were many East Indians, some whose relatives had come to see them off. When she got near the departure area, 'Gatha noticed a young *dougla* woman of about seventeen or eighteen who was saying goodbye to two older East Indian women. It briefly crossed 'Gatha's mind that the young woman of African and East Indian descent, had a *knowing face*. 'Gatha, however, was preoccupied with the minutiae of checking in, and so she paid the young woman little attention. It was apparent that she was related to the older of the two women because there was an obvious family resemblance and she called her "Granny."

"Granny, don't worry," the young woman said in a New York accent. "I'll call you as soon as I get to Queens."

"Ow gyal," the older woman cried. "Me guh miss you too bad. Mus' write and Surojinie guh read it to me. Me eye too bad."

Presumably Surojinie, the other woman nodded vigorously.

'Gatha said goodbye to Leon, hugging him tight, and finding herself sobbing, already feeling him gone. But her tears were as those for a good, close friend, for the father of her children, rather than for a lover. She desperately wanted their parting to be, if not friendly, at least mildly harmonious since there was still the matter of the children to be worked out.

"Gyurl, remembuh dat whatevuh happen, you will always be my chirren mudduh an' I'll always love yuh for dat," he said, tears in his eyes. "If t'ings get bad, come back an' we will see whuh we kyan work out. I sorry, sorry. Give Evadne my sympat'y when yuh see 'er."

"Doan be sorry. Maybe is fuh de bes'. You're a good man, Leon. Is jus' dat I'm not de right woman fuh you. I t'ink you already fine dat woman." She paused to wipe her eyes, taking care not to smudge her mascara. "How you like dis? Boat me an' Evadne losin' we husban's in diff'rent ways."

Long and close, she embraced him for the last time. Then she walked slowly out onto the tarmac. He watched her climb the steps, wave when she got to the top, then finally disappear into the giant metallic bird. She settled herself in a window seat, and when she looked up from fastening her seatbelt, she saw that the young *dougla* woman whom she had seen in the airport, was settling in beside her. They were both *in transit* to Port of Spain, Trinidad.

During the first leg of the flight, 'Gatha learned that her name was Samantha Seelochan. She proved to be very chatty, disclosing that she grew up in Queens and was on her Spring Break from a Richmond Hill high school from which she would soon graduate. She planned to enter Columbia in the fall with a view to going on to Law School later. Interestingly, she planned to specialize in immigration law. She had spent summers, she said, working with her uncle, a Guyanese lawyer in a Richmond Hill law firm and had been bitten by the "law bug" as she put it. She was returning to New York after visiting her ailing maternal grandmother, Rookmin, who lived in Kitty.

"I wasn't born in Guyana," she said. "But because my parents were, I feel so much a part of the place. I love going to see Granny Rook. My parents left the country since 1963, but my mother, (Granny Rookmin's daughter) went into a di-abetic coma and died in New York three years after she and Dad went up. I never knew my mother because I was an in-fant when she died. Just before her death, she left Dad and went to live with her uncle, the lawyer."

A cloud like a promise of Demerara rain passed over her face. She adjusted her seat in the reclining position. 'Gatha suspected that there was *mo in de mawta dan de pistle* regarding her going to live with her uncle, but 'Gatha did not *pick she teet'*. In any event, she herself was quite preoccupied with her own prospects for a return to New York.

"I've seen so much misery on the back of immigration issues that I felt in all good conscience, I had to make it a career—if only to help the people I came from. I know stories that would make your hair curl, but you know, confidentiality and all that," she said importantly.

By the time they changed planes in Port of Spain, both women had gotten to know each other better. 'Gatha told her that she wished to inquire further about an immigration issue on behalf of "a good friend." Samantha was young, but she was developing a lawyer's sense for illegal immigrant anxiety. She shot 'Gatha a knowing look and quickly scribbled her uncle's name and telephone number which she then handed 'Gatha. Samantha also added her own home phone number in the event that 'Gatha would need a further introduction to her Uncle Hanuman. Even as they said goodbye in Port of Spain, 'Gatha still could not shake the feeling that Samantha reminded her of someone she once knew.

CHAPTER SEVENTEEN

'Gatha arrived in Toronto feeling unusually tired and weak. She was surprised when she stood up after the long trip and felt herself getting light-headed, her knees buckling. Her left arm was also slightly numb, causing her to drop her hand luggage twice as she headed to the baggage claim area. For a moment, she felt panicky. She hoped that her health was not deserting her when she most needed it. She could not afford to be sick. She had no medical insurance, no hope of being eligible for it any time soon, and very little money left. She would presently have problems filling a prescription—if she could get one. Fear of detection alone would make her hesitant about going to a doctor's office. She calmed herself thinking that she was probably experiencing the side effects of stress. After all, the last few weeks had not been a barn dance. Some good rest at Gwennie's, she consoled herself, and she would be as good as Mazaruni gold.

She and Gwennie Braithwaite last saw each other eighteen years before. Gwennie was glad to be leaving a miserable existence in Kitty, one punctuated by the actions of a drunken, abusive father who had literally tossed his family out into the street in Kitty when Gwennie was about fifteen. Mercifully, sewing became her salvation when she joined 'Gatha as her *hem-and-stitch gyurl*. In the five years that she worked at this, Gwennie watched helplessly as her ailing mother withered away and her brothers disappeared (as inmates) into the penal Mazaruni mist. Gwennie was always what the village elders called a "nice quiet *gyurl*," always respectful, evoking the maternal sympathies of the neighborhood's older women. When she left Kitty in November 1963, some of them came together, filling in for her mother, outfitting her for the journey to Canada, waving her off at Atkinson.

Gwennie and I were *small gyurls* together, playing littie, and hopscotch, falling out and then in with each other. As the years passed, however, we seemed destined for different lives and so we grew apart.

In the eighteen years since her departure, Gwennie had never returned to the country, not even when her mother died of the mysterious paralysis that crept over her limbs, leaving her sitting uselessly, day in day out, looking out her window onto Lamaha street. Not when early one morning, Gwennie's father was found dead of alcohol poisoning near a trench in Pike Street, just down the road from the village rumshop. Not when her brother, Joe, was stabbed to death in a beer garden fight in Charlotte Street. Soon the village appeared to forget her, but through the years, she and 'Gatha maintained an intermittent correspondence. 'Gatha often wondered aloud how, regardless of the misery she associated with them, Gwennie could so easily turn her back on her family. Then 'Gatha would suck her teeth and say philosophically, "Look—every man to 'e own order, yeh?"

Gwennie's letters to 'Gatha chronicled a life of struggle in Canada, but one that culminated in financial success. At the end of her contractual period of domestic service in Montreal, Gwennie went to work in a dress shop while putting herself through school. She learned French and got a business degree. Years of hard work and dogged persistence paid off when she was put in charge of the dress shop business which she expanded and came to own over the years. In time, she went into other areas of the fashion business opening up three other stores, two of which were in Toronto. At thirty-five, she met and married a French Canadian businessman, Guy

D'Asalines, and they now lived in a fashionable suburb of Toronto.

'Gatha found the change in Gwennie stunning. It was not simply the passage of the years that had wrought the difference; it was the nature of Gwennie's experience. She was glamorous with a quiet sophistication and confidence that belied her earlier image as an anxious, waif-like creature who had posed for *Chronicle* cameraman, Viv McDonald, in a group photo on the Atkinson tarmac in 1963. Indeed, she bore no resemblance to the near destitute girl into whose luggage village women had stuffed guava cheese and Buxton Spice mangoes eighteen years before. 'Gatha realized that they now had little in common. Gwennie's life ('Gatha discovered that everyone called her "Gwen"—Gwen D'Asalines)—was one of ease and comfort. She and Guy often spent their vacations around Mediterranean Europe and the French Caribbean, and seemed to know the "right people."

On the way from the Toronto airport, 'Gatha was eager to impart to her, news and information about the country. Gwennie listened with the kind of polite, detached interest that one reserves for exotic countries which have always excited only mild curiosity. Her struggle in Canada had caused her to develop a focus on careful observation and assessment of people through their actions rather than by means of their words. She had little interest in the kind of gossipy chit-chat into which 'Gatha tended to slip rather easily—the aimless *kya kya kya* as Gwennie would later describe it to me. I suspect that 'Gatha found her somewhat aloof. If Gwennie was so, then I came to understand that it had nothing to do with how she felt about 'Gatha. I believe that her reserve was like the tough shell of an Essequibo turtle, that which enables it to survive the river's ravages. Her aloofness, it appeared, had allowed her to endure (and succeed in) Canadian life.

She was determined to help 'Gatha cross the border into the United States but had no intention of telling Guy what she planned. She figured that if things went wrong and he was later questioned, his denial of culpability would have an unassailable ring of truth. She had no wish to disrupt his life, but she felt impelled to do what she could for 'Gatha. She also knew that if she made him privy to the arrangement, he would do what he could to disrupt it.

Several years after 'Gatha's visit, Gwennie and I met in Toronto during the great annual Caribbean summer festival of *Caribana.* I recognized her as she and Guy stood on the corner of University and Dundas where Guyanese would assemble to meet and greet each other during the festival that attracted hundreds of thousands of Caribbeans. She introduced Guy to me, and he soon went off briefly to explore the festival while she and I renewed old acquaintance in a nearby café.

"Why did you feel the need to help 'Gatha?" I eventually asked her. After all, Gwennie could have offered her some bogus excuse and not endangered her own or her husband's way of life—or she could have flatly refused.

" 'Gatha was one of the few good memories I had of Guyana," Gwennie said simply. Behind her trendy sunglasses, her eyes softened. "She was like Canada to me. She protected and helped me when my own parents and brothers did not. She always gave me of the little she had. I came to love her like my own *sisterblood.* She took me in when she herself was in pain from the loss of her child and a man she loved. How could I *not* help her when she most needed me?"

"But what about your parents and your brother?" I asked. "You never went home to mourn or bury them. It seemed to some in the village that you had deserted them. *They* were your blood."

There followed a pregnant pause and the sound of "Fiah! Fiah!" being belted out by a passing *Caribana* steel band pulsated in the background. A cool, soothing, Canadian summer breeze blew across the hot steel pan sound.

"You knew of my parents only what *you* saw of them," she retorted dryly. "For many years, most often when he came home drunk, my father sexually molested me. Oh... my mother knew about it—almost from the time it started. But she did absolutely nothing to prevent it. I suppose she thought that being so poor, we had no hope of survival without him and so she kept his dirty little secret. Then she started becoming physically paralyzed, and the doctors could find no reason or cure for her condition. Even my brothers knew what was happening to me and they did nothing. His throwing us out was the best thing my father ever did for me."

The pulsating beat of the steel pans intensified.

"In British Guiana of the sixties, who would have helped me? At one point, the country was in racial and political chaos. People were busy murdering each other in the name of race. Child molestation, even by a parent, paled in comparison with obscenities that were occurring then. In any event, what rights did a girl child from a poverty-stricken home have at that time in a country where the police and judicial systems were dominated by men of a certain class? Which authorities could I have gone to? Who would have believed me when even my own family made no move to protect me? Tell me what the hell I owed these people! Tell me! What? What?"

Gwennie was close friends with Marilyn Grimes, a native Trinidadian and Canadian citizen who had migrated to Canada at about the same time she did. For many years, Marilyn worked for Gwennie and Guy as a manager of one of their businesses. However, being a compulsive shopper, Marilyn had accumulated debt which now threatened to bury her. For an undisclosed sum, Gwennie got her to agree to lend her passport to 'Gatha, who was one month younger than she and to whom she bore a striking resemblance. Gwennie told Guy that she would combine the opportunity of dropping 'Gatha off in Buffalo with a chance to shop there and return to Toronto later in the evening. 'Gatha would then take a bus from Buffalo to New York City. Upon her return to Toronto, Gwennie would restore Marilyn's passport to her.

'Gatha had called Jack who said that he would meet her in Buffalo. However, she did not want him to be in her company if anything went wrong with the plan. She insisted that he meet her instead in New York City when she would be hundreds of miles from the border. On the morning of April 15, 1981, Gwennie kissed Guy goodbye, and taking the Gardiner Expressway and the Queen Elizabeth Way, she and 'Gatha set out for the Niagara crossing.

CHAPTER EIGHTEEN

Before they crossed to the United States side, Gwennie took 'Gatha for a brief visit to Niagara Falls. Since they left Toronto, 'Gatha had been feeling tired, and Gwennie felt that a trip to the Falls might pick her up. 'Gatha had never had a real holiday, had not even been able to visit Guyana's magnificent Kaieteur Falls with its own breath-taking drop. On many occasions, Gwennie said, she herself had been touched by the seemingly unearthly power of Niagara, and she had always come away from it feeling strengthened, as she put it— churched. However things turned out, she wanted 'Gatha to take with her the memory of the natural divinity that invested Niagara. 'Gatha was gratified by the side trip and amazed by the Fall's stupendous magnitude, commenting that it was like "starin' right into God face." Gwennie told me that the visit to the Falls seemed to have a strange effect on them both. I think that on the one hand, Niagara was an awesome, but not discouraging, reminder of their insignificance in the universal schema. On the other, it gave them a strange, staggering sense of anticipation and delight, an awareness of their own awesome capacity to endure, as reflected in their past lives, and a relentless determination to face the challenges of the future.

As they approached the reality of the American immigration checkpoint, their earlier buoyancy began to fade. Gwennie became quieter and more alert. The numbness in 'Gatha's left arm returned. She had a suspicion that this was not the first time Gwennie had taken someone across the bridge. She had made 'Gatha learn and recite Marilyn Grimes' personal particulars until 'Gatha almost became dis Marilyn. By means of make-up and hairstyle, she had arranged 'Gatha's appearance to approximate Marilyn's as closely as possible. She even schooled 'Gatha in the Trinidadian accent, instructing her to keep her mouth shut and, when asked a question, to speak only briefly.

"Some people at these checkpoints have been here so long that they can tell the difference between Caribbean accents," Gwennie asserted grimly. "For some reason, though, White officers sometimes have a harder time differentiating between Blacks—especially in photographs. Perhaps it shows that they don't really *want* to see us."

The immigration officer at the end of their line looked like a seasoned veteran in his fifties. Gwennie had hoped that they would be directed to a younger looking woman who worked in the adjacent line, but she had no control over this part of their exit. In any event, it was useless for her to make assessments about people from just a few glances at them. The "veteran" asked for their documents which they immediately proffered.

"What's the reason for your visit to the United States, Mrs. D'Asalines?" he asked, bending down and looking into the driver's side of her Mercedes, his eyes sweeping the car's interior. Unblinkingly, Gwennie met his clear blue eyes.

"My friend and I are going shopping in Buffalo," she responded with a bright, engaging smile—cool as a cucumber in an early Bourda market morning.

"And you, Miss Grimes? Shopping too?" he asked, bending a little lower to get a better look at 'Gatha, his piercing blue eyes attentively going back and forth from her profile to the photograph in the passport he held. Guilt and fear immobilized 'Gatha. She stared straight ahead. Gwennie already answer 'e, she thought. Why de hell 'e 'ave to as' me? 'Gatha's chest tightened with pain and, in the cool Canadian spring, tiny dewlets of sweat began to form on her forehead as her eyes became glassy.

"Miss Grimes?"

Gwennie maintained her cool demeanor.

"Marilyn? Marilyn. He's talking to *you*," she said to 'Gatha, her voice having so slight an edge of urgency that to notice it, you had to have been listening very keenly.

"Y-yes, sir," 'Gatha replied at last. "We goin' to shop. I'm sorry. I'm gettin' a little col'."

"Do you all have anything to declare?" he asked, business-like.

"No we don't," Gwennie replied brightly.

He requested that she open the trunk and he went around to inspect it. As he checked the trunk, 'Gatha started to speak to Gwennie who silenced her by putting her finger to her lips. The officer took both passports inside the little office adjoining the check point and stayed there for a few minutes, during which even the cool Gwennie became a little restless.

"Come on, come *on*, come *on*… , " she whispered, drumming her fingers impatiently on the steering wheel.

Finally, he returned and handed them their passports.

"Welcome to the United States, ladies. Enjoy your stay."

"Oh, we *will*, officer," Gwennie said softly, smiling sweetly up at him. "We will."

In the first moments after they drove away, both women were silent, and then they both *skreeled out* joyfully. They had done it. 'Gatha could not believe that they had now accomplished that which they could earlier only hope for. As they passed them, a couple of motorists shot the women strange looks as though they wondered if the two were driving drunk. With 'Gatha, though, one thought persisted: *"Yuh na dead yet, cuckabeh na pass yuh."*

In Buffalo, she tearfully thanked Gwennie and said goodbye. She thought, "God doan come, but 'e does surely sen'."

Where again would she find a friend as true as this? Then

'Gatha remembered Evadne who had invited her to stay at her home in Queens until she got herself set up again.

As they stood outside the bus station, Gwennie promised, "When you get settled, Guy and I'll come to see you and Evadne. Call me if you need anything."

They embraced and then Gwennie got into her car.

"*Walk good*, gyurl!" Gwennie yelled, darting her friend a last glance and waving just before the car roared off into the night.

Since they met again, it was the first time that 'Gatha heard Gwennie utter a phrase in Creolese.

'Gatha sat in the bus headed out of Buffalo for New York City. The coach ploughed on through the upstate darkness, its rows of seated humanity bouncing and swaying with its movements. From someone's radio, the sound of "I Will Survive," Gloria Gaynor's anthem to endurance, beat low against the night. Some of the passengers hummed the song in low tones as they bobbed their heads to the beat. 'Gatha felt like they were celebrating her success in getting to the other side. Then the mood changed as the sound of "Rivers of Babylon" began to pulse from a player held by one of two Jamaicans sitting behind her.

She considered what she needed to do as soon as she got to New York. Remembering her fellow airline passenger, Samantha Seelochan, 'Gatha checked to make sure she still had her phone number. As soon as 'Gatha got to New York, she resolved that she would contact Samantha's uncle, the Richmond Hills immigration lawyer, Hanuman Singh. She felt she needed to take immediate steps to look into the legal ramifications (and remedies) of her situation. About twenty miles out of the Buffalo bus station, they heard the sound of police sirens. As the bus ground to a halt, many dozing passengers slowly roused themselves.

Through the rear window, 'Gatha could see the flashing police lights. Her chest tightened. The sound of "Rivers of

Babylon" was abruptly shut off. Had she made it this far only to fail again? As she tried to calm herself, she drew resolve from Gwennie's earlier Academy-strength performance at Niagara. The police officer came on board and stood near the driver in the front wheel well. His hazel eyes darted alertly up and down the rows of seats; red eyes in black, brown and white faces stared back at him. Twice, his eyes moved over 'Gatha's damp face, now gleaming in the dim overhead light. She did her best not to meet his gaze, praying that he would not speak to her or ask for identification. She wondered if she was not about to face some kind of horrible retribution for having left her family and taken this desperate risk. *Afta rall, moon a run til daylight kyatch am.*

She sighed with relief when she learned that he had boarded the vehicle only to ticket the driver for going eleven miles over the speed limit. He admonished the driver at some length and then got off. The two Jamaicans seated behind 'Gatha emitted a loud exhalation of relief, and as the bus pulled gingerly away from the shoulder of the road, Jimmy Cliff wailingly resumed:

Oh the wicked carried us away in captivity.
Required from us a song.
But how can we sing King Alpha's song
In a strange land?

Jack met her at the New York Port Authority, and she practically fell into his arms. They were both tearing up with relief that her seemingly interminable journey back to him was over. She wanted to go first to Evadne's, but he protested, saying that he had waited long enough. She agreed to spend the night with him and to proceed to Evadne's the next day. That night, she called Evadne and me from his apartment to let us know that she had made it back, and we all gave a collective, joyful *skreel out*. She also recounted the major details of her trip into the United States from Canada. She told me that on the flight to Port of Spain, she had met a young woman named Samantha Seelochan who reminded her of someone she thought we both knew, but she could not bring the person to mind.

"I was wrackin' my brains tryin' to t'ink who," she said.

In the midst of her telling me about Samantha, she yelled, "Miss Oz! Miss Oz!"

"What *is* your problem, gyurl?" I asked.

"Samantha look like Miss Oz!" 'Gatha said. "But yuh know what? She also resemble yuh ole school frien', Drupattie."

"Gyurl, *guh da side,*" I said. "Nobody en hear from Drupattie in donkey years. You had to much t'rills getting' back to de Big Apple. You mus' be imaginin' t'ings. An' you *know* how racial Miss Oz was. Is hard to imagine dat *she* would have Indian relatives. Dough, yuh nevah kyan tell."

"Look, I gun check yuh-all tomorrow. I got a *lot*ta t'ings to do," she laughed.

The joy and anticipation in her voice were unmistakable.

Like a rabid *rice-eater* prowling through the last few months of her life, coronary artery disease had increasingly stalked Agatha. That night, with a full, full moon rising over the East River, the mangy mongrel sprang, and she suffered a fatal heart attack, dying peacefully as she slept in Jack's arms.

EPILOGUE

Exactly twenty years after these events that I have related to you, I went to a Columbia University alumni get-together in Washington D.C. I had left New York many years before and had since lived near Washington. That afternoon, I looked forward to renewing old acquaintance with students whom I had known closely two decades before. The affair was being held in the heart of downtown Washington and after I found parking, I walked to the venue. It was a gorgeous cherry blossom Spring twilight, the air fresh with the promise of revival and survival, bearing no portent of the destruction that would assail New York later that year.

As we all mingled and chatted, a young woman approached me saying that someone in the group told her I was a Guyanese writer and professor. She said that her parents were also Guyanese and that her name was Samantha Seelochan. It sounded vaguely familiar to me, and I soon realized that it was the name that 'Gatha had recalled to me the night she died. Samantha told me that she had gone to undergraduate at Columbia and then Columbia Law, later passing the bar. As an immigration law specialist with responsibility for Caribbean immigrant matters, she worked in the Washington office of a Queens, New York congressman. She could not recall her meeting with 'Gatha but politely inquired about her anyway.

"She died the night she returned to New York," I replied. "She had hoped to see your uncle about her immigrant status—or lack of it. After she died, we found your uncle's card and your telephone number in her hand bag. She seemed bent on getting in touch with you all."

There was a pause and then she said, "My uncle told me that he believed my mother knew you. Her name was Drupattie. He said you both went through High School together."

Drupattie, a young East Indian woman, and I had been close friends in high school, but I never saw her again after she suddenly left school. I was pleasantly surprised to discover who Samantha was and had many questions about her mother, but we could not talk at length during the alumni social, so we arranged to meet in a few days at a Union Station café near Capitol Hill.

In Guyana, during the racial unrest of the early sixties, Drupattie had fallen in love with a young Black Guyanese, named Steven Osbourne. We had all grown up together. For racist reasons, both Steven's mother, Miss Oz, and Drupattie's uncle, Balgobin, were dead set against the relationship with which Steven and Drupattie persisted in spite of the opposition. Balgobin then took Drupattie out of school and married her off to Ramdat Seelochan, the son of a prosperous Courentyne rice mill owner of whom Drupattie had no prior acquaintance. Her plans to go to medical school were thus dashed. She had no viable alternatives because her father had just died; she was very young; and she and her mother were destitute. In an action which it was assumed Balgobin instigated, a group of Indian men viciously attacked Steven in Thomas Lands, landing him in hospital. Smarting from the assault, Steven soon left the country to study in England. By this time, Drupattie had departed for the Courentyne, with her new, stunningly unfamiliar husband.

Samantha put her arm through mine and guided me to an expensive, trendy Station café where she insisted on treating me. As I was for her, so was she full of questions for me, queries about her mother and what she was like as a young woman.

Then she told me what she knew of her mother's story. As the racial hostilities intensified on the Courentyne, Ramdat decided that he and Drupattie would relocate to Queens where his brothers had already gone. In the early sixties, according to Samantha, it was easier to immigrate. Ramdat was a skilled mechanic, and he was hired to work in a small car repair business that one of his brothers owned.

Samantha said that by the time they got to the States, Ramdat and Drupattie realized they had a serious problem. Not only was Drupattie pregnant, but all indications pointed to the fact that the child could not possibly be her husband's. Ramdat was furious. He considered dat 'e was fooled into *buyin' pig in bag*. He felt duped not only by Balgobin but also by Drupattie, and in fits of violent rages, he began beating her. Barefoot and pregnant, Drupattie was forced to flee one night to the Richmond Hill home of her father's youngest brother, Hanuman, then a young law student and part-time taxi-driver. There she and Samantha stayed. In spite of the fact that Drupattie never divulged to Hanuman and his family the identity of her child's father and despite the child's *dougla* appearance, Hanuman's support and love for them both never wavered.

"Uncle Hanuman *was* my true-true father," Samantha said, using the Creole expression.

Drupattie had inherited her father's diabetes, compromising her ability to work and impairing her vision, kidney function and circulation. By the time that Samantha was three, Drupattie was dead of diabetic complications. She never disclosed the name of Samantha's father.

As well as wanting to find out what her mother was like, Samantha also wanted to know if I had any idea of who her father was. None of her family in Guyana wanted to tell her. They said the man had left the country many years before, and they had no idea where he had gone. As far as they were concerned, he might well be dead.

'Gatha was right. She did *fayva* Miss Oz *bad bad*. I did not tell her that about ten years before in Washington, I had encountered Steven Osbourne, the man I assumed to be her father. Or that intermittently through the years, I had been in touch with him.

The next day, I called him at his London home, told him about Samantha, and asked whether he wanted me to give her his contact information. He was happily stunned

"What about Drew," he asked. "Where is she?"

"She died years ago," I replied gently and told him the circumstances as Samantha related them to me.

At the other end of the line, there was silence— then he began to sob. In all these years, he had been twice divorced, and his last wife had suffered two miscarriages. I don't think he ever stopped hoping that he would be with Drupattie again.

"Just when I thought I had no children—" he laughed-cried. "If she *is* ours, for us Samantha may be the one good thing to come out of all the racism and sexism of the time," he said.

"I hope your instincts are right," he continued. "In two days, I have to fly to New York on business. I'll take a couple of days off and come down to Washington immediately."

Afta rall, na tek yuh mattie eye fuh see.

"Don't worry. She would have made Drew proud. *You'*ll like her too," I added.

Samantha met us in Union Station and took us to the same trendy bistro where she and I had first gone. She and Steven could not stop talking to each other. There were too many years to cover. Their laughter rose intermittently over the hum of the crowd After a while, I felt happily superfluous and made an excuse to go.

Walking through the crowds in historic Union Station, always silent witness to a gamut of human emotion, I realized that in the years since I met Agatha again, the sound of the train no longer reminded me of destruction. I thought of her life and those of Eunice, Drupattie and Compton, all now gone to their ancestors, each bearing a full *kyalabash*. As I emerged into the Massachusetts Avenue sunshine, I felt certain that happiness and human dignity have more to do with how one negotiates the journey rather than on what waits at its end.

Na everyt'ing schola know, 'e learn from teacha.

Glossary of Guyanese Colloquial Terms

PAGE

1. *"Hungry daag a nyam kyalabash":* Desperation leads people to take unusual measures.
4. *Limers:* those who hang around a location
4. *Called off:* calling out to (the verbal equivalent of 'whistling at')
4. *Tackled:* made romantic approaches to
6. *Write home:* propose marriage. A suitor would write a letter to the head of a household asking for a daughter's hand in marriage, extolling her virtues, and describing his ability to provide materially.
6. *I'se me own big woman:* I am independent.
7. *Spit press:* Gossip mill
7. *"Yuh na dead yet, cuckabeh na pass yuh":* Living renders one vulnerable to disaster.
7. *Tantalized:* teased
8. *Playin' great, smellin' sheself:* being snobbish and over-ambitious
8. *Full mout':* disrespectful address to someone (particularly an older person) by her first name only
8. *Dajeuners:* festive lunches (from the French, *déjeuner*)
9. *She one an' God:* She alone
9. *Wouldn' pick 'er teet':* made no comment
11. *Every skin teet' na laugh:* A person's outwardly cheerful response may be deceptive.

15. *Puckaterry:* trouble (purgatory)
15. *At the foot of the cross:* in God's hands
16. *God doan come, but 'e does sen':* Prayer may be answered indirectly.
17. *Kitta Katta:* little by little
19. *Whuh is joke fuh small boy is det fuh crapaud:* What is mere diversion for one person may be a serious detriment to someone else.
19. *Steupsing:* indicating irritation by making a sucking sound with the teeth and tongue
19. *On the back of it:* in addition to that
21. *Nennen:* godmother
22. *Child fathers:* unmarried fathers of children
25. *Stan':* looks like
27. *Beg a lodgin':* seek shelter
30. *"When man done such cane, 'e dash peelin' pun grung":* People are quick to discard that which no longer serves their purpose.
34. *Sweet man:* a man whose financial needs are met solely by a woman or by women
36. *Kyat eat yuh dinner:* you lose
36. *Rice Eaters:* stray dogs
37. *Boat gone a falls:* The situation is irretrievable.
38. *Woman alone like kyalabash: Ev'rybody wan pass an' dip dey han' ":* Single women are vulnerable to the guile of all who would prey on them.
38. *Nineted:* rubbed down (anointed)
39. *De mudflat:* a sometime reference to the coastlands
40. *Fawwud:* forward, presumptuous
42. *Favor him bad:* resembles him closely
45. *Hurry-up hurry-up:* hurriedly, not well thought out
46. *Fufu:* pounded plantains
47. *Mawga:* skinny
56. *Wrong an' strong:* adamant in defending one's position even when one is mistaken

59. *Two big 'oman kyan live in de same house:* It is impossible for two independent women to co-exist in the same dwelling.
60. *Tek she eye an' pass me:* showed me disrespect
61. *T'rowin' remarks:* making none too subtle disparaging remarks
65. *Ketch sheself:* recover
65. *Dat breeze cun pass between dem:* close
66. *Small piece:* pocket money
66. *Fine somet'ing to do:* get a job
77. *Step out of her crease:* be presumptuous (an allusion to cricket)
82. *Disgustin':* annoying
83. *Eyepass:* disrespect
85. *Is mo in de mawta dan de pistle:* There is more to this situation than appears.
86. *Givin' me blow:* being unfaithful
86. *"Teet' an' tongue mus' bite":* Friction occurs in any relationship.
86. *Bear an' forbear:* be patient
86. *"Do suh na like suh":* Those who inflict pain on others dislike being on the receiving end of similar treatment.
90. *Fatigue:* tire out by persistent, unwelcome interrogation or requests
95. *Idocity:* audacity
96. *Boviander:* a person of Amerindian and other racial mixture
102. *Dayclean:* early morning
104. *Mickase:* make haste
104. *Sunhot:* the hot mid-afternoon
105. *Grass corner:* grassy edge of road
106. *Rass:* (Expletive)
106. *Suck salt:* be in desperate need
107. *Eye was kyatchin' fyah:* was becoming attracted
113. *Tricky and tranney:* two people who are being cagey with each other

113. *Camoudi:* snake
113. *Hang his hat:* having all his financial needs met by a woman. (Behaving like a *sweet man*)
116. *Hyse up yuh frack an' buse:* ignorant and contentious while lacking self-respect
119. *Walk with:* bring
121. *Flatform:* platform
126. *Chief cook and bottle-washer:* person who has taken control of a situation
126. *Skreeled out:* screamed
127. *"Han' wash han' mek han' come clean":* By working cooperatively with others, one helps oneself.
131. *"Pickney who a cry a house an' a door a same t'ing:"* The general implication of this is that "parents should extend to other people's children the same regard they award their own."
132. *"Good kyalabash na a float a ribba":* Stable attitudes afford people solid lives. Another interpretation of this saying is: "Single people who have not found partners are in some way defective."
134. *A knowing face:* familiar countenance
139. *Kya kya kya:* idle laughter
146. *Walk good:* good luck
147. *"Moon a run till daylight kyatch am":* You can run but you can't hide.
148. *"Guh da side":* "Get outa here."
149. *Drupattie:* Years after I had written *The Coloured Girl in the Ring*, I spoke to Rochika Chaudhry, a New Delhi native, who drew my attention to the significance of Draupadi in Hindu mythological lore. When I first wrote about Drupattie, Draupadi's Guyanese counterpart by name in *The Coloured Girl,* I had not been familiar with the myth of Draupadi. I was surprised to find that the mythological Draupadi bore some resemblance to the Drupattie of my own creation in *The*

Coloured Girl and in *Calabash Parkway*: Draupadi is the subject of a feud between two groups, the Pandyas and Kauravs, the latter of whom eventually win her. Interestingly, in *Calabash Parkway,* Drupattie's recuer, her Uncle Hanuman, has the name of the Hindu god who is noted for his courage, power, faithfulness and selfless service.

151. *Buyin' pig in bag:* being deceived
152. *"Na tek yuh mattie eye fuh see":* Do not accept unreservedly other people's description of circumstances.
153. *"Na everyt'ing schola know, 'e learn from teacha":* Experience affords lessons that are not acquired in a classroom.